The Boy on the Ox's Back
and other African Legends

The Boy

on the Ox's Back

and other African Legends

FORBES STUART

Illustrated by
JOHN LAWRENCE

HAMISH HAMILTON

First published in Great Britain 1971
by Hamish Hamilton Children's Books Ltd
90 Great Russell Street, London W.C.1

© Forbes Stuart 1971
Illustrations © John Lawrence 1971

S B N 241 01970 2

Dedicated to Lara and Audrey and
the Staff of the British Museum
Reading Room

Printed in Great Britain by
Western Printing Services Ltd, Bristol

Contents

5

Contents

Introduction

The stories in this collection come from all over Africa, as far north as the Gold Coast and the Sudan, as far south as the Cape Province, taking in a multitude of African peoples. Because two-thirds of the Africans speak Bantu languages, a number of stories in this book have Bantu origins, while others represent some of the hundreds of non-Bantu tribes.

Eighteen stories can form no more than an introduction to African Folklore. About seven thousand stories have appeared in print (mostly in academic books and journals), but collectors estimate that the figure for *unrecorded* African folktales may run as high as 200,000. Many of the stories are the merest anecdotes, but the best ones are so beautifully formed and so universal that they more than survive comparison with the folklore of the most sophisticated communities in the world.

The origins of most of these tales are, of course, hidden in antiquity. For untold centuries they have been passed from one generation to the next by word of mouth, and it wasn't until about ninety years ago that anthropologists, travellers, government officials and missionaries began to take down these legends from tribal storytellers and translate them into English, French, and German.

In collecting the material for these stories, I have gone back mainly to nineteenth-century translations which are often artless and literal and retain the endless repetitions that African storytellers indulged in while telling their tales around the campfire, emphasising dramatic highlights with gestures, at times with a chant. Because the storytellers were *creative* raconteurs, many a tale will differ greatly from area to area, and I have on occasion used material from a number of variants to make up one story for this book.

Ignoring the myths and legends that tell of the Creator, the formation of the world, the birth of the tribe, migrations and warfare, I have concentrated on tales about people and animals, staying as close to the original story-line as possible but writing them in a style that is my own. Too many Western writers have faltered through giving their heroes a vulgarised "Brer Rabbit" dialect or peppering their refurbishings of African legends with indigenous proverbs (of which the Ashanti alone have at least 3600!).

Joel Chandler Harris's celebrated "Brer Rabbit" came to the United States via the slaves imported from the Gold Coast, and no less an authority than Alice Werner claimed in MYTHS AND LEGENDS OF THE BANTU (1933) that "it seems quite likely that our Aesop's Fables originated in Africa". She says that Luqman (the Arab fabulist praised by Mohammed in the 31st chapter of the Koran) seems to have been a Negro slave, an "Ethiopian". From North Africa his stories travelled to Greece, "where he was known as Aithiops, and this was taken to be his name and turned into Aesop."

The hare that features so largely in Bantu folklore became Brer Rabbit in the New World. The spider from Gold Coast folklore (see SPIDER AND ELEPHANT AND HIPPO) is the Anansi known to slave descendants in Jamaica and Guyana, and called Aunt Nancy by the Gullah of South Carolina whose forefathers were African slaves. Cuba had its quota of slaves as well, and in Cuban folklore to this day the tortoise is as brilliant and mercurial and quite as shrewd as the tortoise who cavorts through THE GHOST OF THE MIGHTY TOROFINI.

The stories about people tell of chief's sons marrying beautiful princesses, little girls escaping from giant ogres with the help of a good witch (although there are wicked ones as well), and heroes turning into animals as the young man does in KING OF THE EARTH AND THE WATER.

Very often there is a moral, not usually explicitly stated as it is in Aesop, but *implied* through the success or failures of the characters. Only certain tribes, like the Chagga on the southern slopes of Mount Kilimanjaro, tailor their folklore to educational requirements. In most cases the words of William J. Thomas—who coined the term *Folklore* in 1846—apply: "It includes everything that relates to the ancient traditions, beliefs, observances,

9

customs and superstitions of the ordinary population."

The eighteen stories in this book come from communities in Africa that range from small village-based hunting bands to highly organised states, some subscribing to the divine right of kings. African folklore gives us an insight into the many qualities of man as seen through a poetical mind. The widespread Bantu-language stories especially express a sense of unity and a shared culture.

But above all they are entertaining and give full scope to all the human emotions.

FORBES STUART, *London,* 1970

The Goat Who Turned Somersaults

This story combines two goat legends that come from the Mpongwes, part of the Hausa tribe of five million inhabiting Equatorial West Africa.

Late in the nineteenth century these legends were written down in English by an anthropologist at the town of Libreville on the Gaboon River, and were first published in R. S. Rattray's scholarly work on Hausa Folklore in 1913.

A long time ago, before lions and hyenas and leopards began to live in the bush, a goat decided to build himself a new home. Choosing the place, he went to seek the posts around which he would build.

When he brought the timber to the site next morning he was pleasantly surprised to find the ground already cleared. "What considerate neighbours there must be in these parts," he thought as he planted the posts and dug the foundations. Every day until the house was completed he found that someone else had been working on it during the night. Soon a fine four-roomed house stood in the clearing, ready to accommodate himself, his wife, and his three children.

Dismay came when they moved in next morning, for three of the four rooms were occupied by a lion, a hyena, and a jackal! The goat's wife was terrified, so were his children, but he remained calm, knowing that the other animals had not seen a goat before. So he strutted about arrogantly and seemingly unafraid, making aggressive movements with his horns, and then listened hard during the night as the lion, hyena and jackal whispered hoarsely to one another.

The jackal said: "I have never seen such an animal before. What is it? Where does he come from? He has a fine pair of horns, but if we moved in on him together we could kill him and eat the whole family."

The lion said: "Let us be circumspect and bide our time. He looks very strong and fierce to me, and he may destroy us all if we provoke him. In any case, there is much game and plenty of good eating in these parts, so we won't go hungry if we leave him alone for the time being."

The hyena said: "Listen to my plan. We'll tell him that we as a community have decided that each one of us should be responsible for bringing in food. First you, lion, will hunt for food, then the jackal, then myself; and on the fourth day we shall find out whether he is able to hunt and kill. If he fails, why, into the pot with him!" They laughed so much at their own cunning that the wall against which the goat was holding his ear trembled and shook, and so did he.

Three days went by. Each day one of the animals brought home the food he had hunted and killed— a buck, a zebra, and an okapi. "Off you go," they said to the goat on the fourth morning. "You must be the provider today." And although he marched bravely into the bush, shaking his horns menacingly, the goat was miserable and afraid, for was he not always the hunted one and never the killer? But he searched and searched until he was too weary to go any farther, then lay down in the shade of a mighty baobab tree to gather back his strength. By then it was late afternoon.

Out of the corner of his eye he saw an eagle flap down on the topmost branch of that baobab tree. With pounding heart the goat held his breath and pretended to be dead, fooling the big bird of prey so successfully that the eagle swooped down upon him. But the goat grabbed and held him so fiercely that he pleaded for mercy: "Let me be free to soar back into the sky and I shall give you a charm that will make it possible for you to destroy animals much bigger than yourself. But first you must promise to let me go."

The goat agreed and the eagle continued: "Pluck out four of my feathers, white ones only, place them between the toes of your right foot— the magic will not work on the left—and when you see an animal, walk behind it, do a somersault, then let it run a little way, and your next somersault will kill your prey." The goat plucked the feathers and the eagle flew away, wheeling in great circles with the joy of still being alive until it was no bigger than a black dot against the blue of the late afternoon sky.

The magic worked! A hartebeest lay dead on the plain and the goat fetched his neighbours and took them to the animal as the sun was setting. "It's too big for me to drag home," he said.

Later that night the lion said, "He's a killer. I'm glad we left him alone." But the hyena said: "He is so small and the hartebeest so large that he must have had help, and I shall keep my eye on him."

Four days later the goat's turn to provide the communal meal came again. From bush to bush, from tree to tree, the hyena slunk behind him. He saw the goat doing something to his right paw (he wasn't near enough to make out exactly what) and watched him sidle up behind a giraffe stretching its neck into the branches of a high tree to nibble the succulent leaves. The goat turned head-over-heels,

14

the startled giraffe loped clumsily away on its long legs; then the hyena saw the goat do another somersault and the dustcloud rose into the treetops as the animal fell to the ground with a crash. The hyena trembled in fear. And at that moment the goat saw him.

"Ah, hyena," he nodded jovially, "see our evening meal! Let's go home and get the lion and jackal to help us drag it to our house." The two neighbours trotted away, the sun throwing long shadows in front of them. Occasionally the hyena would see the shadow next to his getting shorter as the goat fell back, and panic-stricken he would leap to one side, crying, "Do not follow me! Do not walk behind me! It makes me nervous." And the goat chuckled quietly because he knew that the hyena had seen how he had killed the giraffe. "Wait until night comes," he thought. "That will be the time for decisions to be made and implemented."

"Two somersaults, that was all, and the giraffe died by magic," said the hyena. "And then, on the way home, with the sun behind us, I could see his shadow getting shorter and I knew he was somewhere behind me. I was never so terrified in my life."

The lion said: "Yes, he is a dangerous fellow. I, of course, fear no animal, but I must admit that magic tends to make me lose some of my courage because I feel so helpless against it, you understand."

The jackal said: "That little animal could kill us all, one at a time or all three together, depending on his mood at the time. Any other animal we can destroy, but this stranger is too much for us." Listening at the wall, the goat heard his three terrified neighbours making their decision: "We'll have to live in the bush, for if we build another house he could sneak up and lie in wait for us."

The three animals tiptoed out of the house and into the night, to live in the bush, as they have done ever since; and next morning the goat's three children took over their rooms.

*

Years later, long after the goat with the magic gift of killing by turning somersaults had died, his descendants lived in fear and trembling because they were unprotected—except by their reputation —against the teeth and claws of wild animals. But one day a goat came home to his wife so excited that he could barely speak.

"I cannot tell you who or what or how, but I have been given the power to defeat any animal I care to wrestle with. Even the elephant will be no match for me. I can become the wrestling champion of all Africa, and goats will be feared and respected again." He went to sleep that night dreaming of a wrestling marathon in which he wrestled with the animals one by one and vanquished them all.

News gets around very swiftly in the bush. A chatter here, a hiss there, a growl in a clearing, a baboon swinging from tree to tree with the story, and every animal is informed. Within a few days the challengers began to arrive at the goat's house. They called him boaster, upstart, braggart, liar, pretender, impostor, and he wrestled with them all and defeated them—antelopes, lions, elephants, quaggas, all of them, with the exception of the leopard who was the last to hear of the goat's prowess.

Storming up to the goat's house, he roared: "I don't believe a word of it! I could wrestle you into the dust and eat your whole tribe for breakfast. Come! The mighty leopard is eager to demolish you and destroy these foolish unfounded rumours of your wrestling prowess. Die, goat!"

But when the dust settled, the leopard was slinking away, abjectly humiliated but fiercely angry. He slunk down to the spring where the goat always drank so that he could ambush and kill his victor. He was so incensed that when two men from the nearby kraal came to drink he sprang upon them and killed them. And the story was passed on by growl and grunt and hiss and chatter until it came to the ears of the goat: "The leopard is killing men because of you."

Because the goat feared for his wife's safety, he took her with him to where his uncle the antelope lived. "You stay here," said the antelope, "and I'll find a way of dealing with the leopard." Three days later the goat and his wife hid themselves just as the leopard ran up to the antelope and roared, "Where is the goat who wrestles?"

"What has my neighbour done to enrage you so?"

"He has humiliated me and he must die!" And with these words the leopard grabbed the antelope and hissed at him: "Show me where the goat and his wife are hiding or you will die in their place." Terrified, the antelope whispered, "Come tonight and I will reveal their sleeping place. Kill them, leopard, by all means, but leave me in peace, for I have not incurred your wrath."

But the goat overheard his uncle's promise of betrayal and fled with his wife to the home of the elephant and told him what had happened. While the elephant was telling them how much he admired a skilful wrestler, the news of the antelope's death reached them. The elephant hid them, defied the leopard, and was killed. And the trail of death continued. Every animal helping the goat was killed by the leopard. The zebra perished, the jackal and the giraffe. Each time the goat and his wife managed to escape, but they were becoming worn out through being continually hunted by their implacable enemy.

One day the goat's wife said: "My husband, we are exhausted. We cannot keep this up for ever. Soon the leopard must catch up with us, but in the meanwhile he will kill every animal who helps or shelters us, until the animals themselves turn on us in their terror. Now, I have a plan. Let us go to where men live and see if they will let us stay with them."

The goat agreed, and man took them to his kraal

and gave them a house to live in, saying, "You are safe here. Go in peace." And when the leopard came to that place seeking them, man admonished him: "The animals you killed could not retaliate, but we can. We have great powers. If you continue to hunt the goats, who are now in our care, you will surely die. Begone!"

But the leopard snarled in reply that he would hunt them until he caught and killed them, and one night soon afterwards, when the moon was down and darkness complete, he sprang over the wooden wall that enclosed the kraal, and sniffing the musky aroma of the goat he crept towards the house, and slid into the doorway, the odour of the goat tantalising his nostrils. But even as he cried out, "Now you die, goat!" he was killed by the men who had set a trap for him, ambushing him by lying in wait in the front room while the goat and his wife were safe in the back.

At sunrise the goat and his wife thanked the men of the village for saving them from the leopard's wrath and prepared to go back to the bush, but the headman of the village said, "You will never be safe out there. You will always be fleeing from one leopard or another, and you cannot escape them always. Stay with us where the grass is green and succulent bushes grow in abundance, and we will protect you and all goats who come after you."

And ever since that day the goats have lived with man as domestic animals.

Spider and Elephant and Hippo

First recorded in Northern Nigeria, this tale comes from the Hausas, many of whom live on the Gold Coast. Renowned as traders and artisans, farmers and stockbreeders, they were politically powerful in the Middle Ages, and were converted to Mohammedanism by Arab traders who also taught them to use Arabic script.

Because their trading expeditions brought them in contact with all the West African tribes, it is not surprising to find the story of SPIDER AND ELEPHANT AND HIPPO in their folklore. Usually featuring a tortoise or a hare instead of a spider, it appears in many tribes, including the widespread Bantu; but the Hausa version is the most imaginative one.

Because there was a famine in the land, the spider and his family grew thinner and thinner and hungrier and hungrier. In his desperation the spider said to his wife: "Here we are, starving, while the elephant and hippo have stored away much grain for these lean times. The big ones have, the little ones have not, but tomorrow we shall have our share."

At sunrise the spider spoke with the elephant: "Great land animal, king wherever you walk on the earth, I come to you as a messenger from the hippo. The King of the Water requests you to deliver one hundred baskets of grain to the river's edge, in exchange for which he will give you a fine horse when the harvest comes again. But none of the lowlier animals must hear of this transaction which is a matter only for kings. This evening when the sun goes down, may it please your majesty?"

That evening the young elephants deposited one hundred bags of grain on the riverbank. The spider thanked them, and said he would tell the hippo to collect them; but no sooner had the elephants tramped off into the bush than his own family swarmed on to the riverbank to carry the grain home with them. That night the spider family and all their relatives and friends ate until their bodies were bulging, but the spider was still not content.

With the morning sun bounding into the African sky, he appeared on the riverbank to address the hippo: "Great water animal, king wherever you go

21

in the river, I come to you as a messenger from the elephant. The King of the Land has much grain but is in need of fish to make soup, so he requests you to deliver one hundred baskets of fish to the river's edge, in return for which he will give you a fine horse when the harvest comes again. But none of the lowlier animals must hear of the transaction which is a matter only for kings. This evening when the sun is going down, may it please your majesty?"

That evening the young hippos placed one hundred baskets of fish on the riverbank, and as soon as they had splashed back into the river, the bubbles breaking on the surface above their heads, hordes of spiders scuttled down to the water's edge to drag the fish away. Again there was a night of carousing and guzzling, and shortly before the sun came up the spider addressed his family and friends: "Listen," he said, "for two nights we have driven our hunger away, and there is enough left over for many nights to come. But the famine will not last for ever, and one day we shall be called upon to pay for all this lovely food. So I must ask you to plait a long thick rope, as thick as a cobra and as long as from here to Bajimso. And here is my plan." When he had told them, they rolled about laughing, and small groups of them danced like tiny dervishes in their glee.

The rains came, the fields waved with grain, and the famine was only a memory, when the elephant sent for the spider and demanded his fine horse. The spider said he would talk with the hippo and return on the day after the next. The spider's family and friends helped him to drag the long rope to a very thick baobab tree.

Tying one end securely round the tree, he pulled the other end through the jungle and handed it to the elephant. "Here is a rope, King of the Land. Tomorrow the King of the Water will tie the horse —which is still wild and untamed—to the other end of the rope; in the meanwhile you must attach your end to a strong tree. At dawn, when the tree shakes, let all young elephants pull for all they are worth so that the horse will be brought to you."

Then he went to the hippo, saying that the elephant had kept his promise of a gift of a fine horse, but as a spider's strength was not sufficient to pull a horse, especially such a wild and untamed one, he had fastened the rope to a baobab tree. "At dawn, let your young hippos unfasten the rope and pull for all they are worth so that the horse will be brought to you."

When the elephants saw the branches of the tree shaking in the dawn and the leaves dancing, they untied the rope and pulled with all their combined strength. But the hippos were pulling with all theirs, and neither side moved backwards or forwards while the sun rose in the morning and set at the end of the day, and elephants and hippos lay down utterly exhausted and slept where they fell.

On the next day they tried again, with as little

success. "Tie the rope to a tree," said the elephant, and far away the hippo said the same.

Next morning the elephant and the hippo met halfway, each one nearly bursting with rage. "I've come to ask you what kind of a horse it is that can keep my young hippos pulling and straining in vain for two whole days," bellowed the hippo.

"That's exactly what I've come to see you about," replied the angry elephant.

When they realised that they had been engaged in a fruitless and exhausting tug-of-war, that there was no horse and that the crafty spider had tricked each of them in turn, they vowed to catch and punish the tiny rogue. But the spider went into hiding, afraid to show himself, growing thin and weak until he had to emerge—or die of hunger.

Staggering along, looking for food, he found an antelope hide, complete with hoofs and head, and crawled under it just as the elephant crashed through the trees and lumbered into the clearing. His cunning brain working swiftly, he asked, "O mighty elephant, are you looking for the spider? Look what he has done to me, until recently an antelope in my prime. We had an argument, and look what he has done to me."

The elephant cried, "Do you mean to say that the spider made you so frail and weak? But how? How?"

"He pointed at me, that was all, and my health and strength drained out of me, but, please, do not mention this to anybody, for I do not want him to come again. Next time he will surely destroy me completely. Oh, the power of that tiny insect!"

"Certainly," stammered the elephant, "on condition that you promise not to tell him that I am looking for him." And as he turned to go, the spider came out into the open, saying, "Elephant, I believe you are seeking me."

As the elephant protested, the spider said, "If I hear again that you are looking for me, you will share the fate of the unfortunate antelope who was misguided enough to argue with me."

After the elephant had fled, the spider's strength returned with some food he found, and he scurried under the antelope's hide just as the hippo emerged snorting under the trees. "How feeble and decrepit you look, antelope. Whatever has happened to reduce you to such a state?"

"Do not mention it to anybody because I do not want to suffer still further, but I was foolish enough to involve myself in an argument with the spider. He pointed at me and I withered away. So small he is, but so powerful. But how was I to know that until I fell victim to his spell!"

"Well," said the hippo in alarm, "there is no need to mention that I am looking for him, or should I say *was* looking for him. That will be our little secret, antelope, and I hope your recovery will be swift and complete."

He turned to go, and the spider came out, saying,

"Hippo, it is said in the forest that you are looking for me. Well, here I am!"

"Rumours, my dear fellow, rumours, unfounded at that," blurted the hippo. "What have *you* ever done to me, eh, that I should be seeking you? No, dear little friend, I am not looking for you, just out for a quiet stroll. But now I must get back to my family. Goodbye, spider!"

And the spider laughed to hear the hippo blundering into trees in his panic, and finally hurling himself into the river with a splash that could be heard as far away as Bajimso.

26

Gratitude

The collector Frobenius took this folktale down when he visited the Nupe tribe in the Sudan. The Nupe who live in grass-thatched huts of mud brick, are farmers, but their guild system for craftsmen is highly organised. The tribe of about 360,000 people embraced Mohammedanism, and the moralising conclusion of GRATITUDE reflects the influence of Islam on the Nupe.

The bow twanged. The arrow struck. The antelope was dead. As the hunter who had been stalking his victim through the bush all morning walked towards the fallen animal, a jackal spoke from behind a tree: "For two days now I have prowled in vain, and my hunger conquers my fear of you, and when you need me I shall help you, for one favour begets another, and as we treat others so shall we ourselves be treated."

Because his mood was jovial and there was an abundance of meat, the hunter gave some to Boaji the jackal, not expecting any favours in return, for how can a little jackal possibly be of any help to a mighty hunter?

On the following day, deep in the bush, a sudden rustling made him tense and a crocodile emerged from the long grass, shaking and sobbing, his tears falling. Having no fear for the river-animal on dry land, the hunter asked him what he was doing there so far from the river his home.

"I am lost and cannot find my way home after two days in the bush where I have been hunting without success. If you know the way to the river, lead me there and I promise to give you five baskets of fish." Tying a leather thong to the crocodile's leg, the hunter led him through the bush to the banks of the River Niger, one of the greatest waterways in Africa, and waited there while the grateful crocodile slid through the water to fetch the baskets of fish. He brought them one at a time, placing each one nearer to the river's edge and the fifth basket in the shallow water. When the unsuspecting hunter was in the water up to his knees the crocodile grabbed him and swam swiftly to a sandbank in the middle of the turbulent river, the dry land far away, and flung him on to the sand.

Before the hunter could open his mouth in protest, thirty crocodiles surrounded him, some on the sandbank clashing their jaws together, others circling hungrily in the water. The treacherous animal who had captured him said to the circle of crocodiles: "Friends, I have brought you a hunter. He is defenceless. His bow and poison-tipped arrows lie useless on the riverbank. I shall kill him, we shall eat him, and to round off our meal there are five baskets of fish that the hunter will have no further use for." And he moved towards the man.

"Stop!" cried the hunter. "Let me speak before I die. Your friend was lost, sobbing in the bush far from the Niger. He begged for my help and I gave it to him, making no attempt to kill him when he was at my mercy but bringing him back to his family and his friends in the river. Now he wants to have me eaten. Is this justice? Is that gratitude?"

The hunter's impassioned words sent the crocodiles into a debating huddle from which the treacherous one emerged to say that they had decided to discuss the matter with the first four river-users to come their way; and it wasn't long before an old mat, frayed and tattered, came floating down the river to be pushed against the sandbank by the swift current.

"Asubi, help me in my need!"

"What has taken the smile from your face, hunting man?"

When he had listened to the hunter's story, the
old mat spoke before drifting away down the river:

"When I was new men kept me clean,
Swept off my dust and I stayed green.
How fine I was, so brightly beaded,
Rolled up when I wasn't needed.
But age defaced me;
They replaced me
And threw me in the river.

"Crocodiles, I commend your eating plan,
And advise you now to treat this man
As his fellows treated me—
Old oval mat Asubi!"

The crocodiles were still chuckling gleefully
when a discarded dress, torn and faded, was washed
up on the sandbank, to listen to the hunter's plea
and make reply before moving away through the
water towards the faraway sea:

"They tossed me away when I was old.
Gone the blue and the shining gold
That made a woman lovelier then,
Admired by all the handsome men
Who praised her loveliness divine
When they should have been praising mine!
Discarded now and in the river,
Would I help a young man?—Never!"

The hunter was in despair, but his hopes rose
again when an old horse, thin with ribs showing,

staggered down to the river to drink. "Friend of man," he shouted, "help me in my trouble. I beseech you." And cupping his hands he cried out his story. He and the crocodiles could just make out the horse's reply across the wide expanse of water:

"Not fair, I hear you cry, Not fair!
But I am an old rejected mare
Who served my masters for my share
Of grass and grain,
Kindness, care,
Shelter from the slanting rain.

"But when I became too old to bear
(my foals one day will follow me here)
Their sticks came whistling through the air
To drive me away to die in my pain—
I'll never help a man again!"

The hunter gave himself up for lost. Only one more chance. Then he saw a small animal trotting towards the riverbank. Boaji the jackal! A friend at last!

"Help me, Boaji, as you said you would."

"I cannot hear you very well. Ask a crocodile to come over here and carry me to the sandbank on his back so that we can talk without having to shout."

No sooner said than done, and Boaji asked the hunter to tell him what had happened. When he had finished the crocodiles shouted confidently for a

31

verdict in their favour but the jackal replied, "A decision cannot be made until I hear both sides of the story. Crocodile, tell me how the hunter guided you back to the river." The crocodile explained how the hunter had bound a leather thong to his leg and led him through the bush back to the river; and the jackal said he could make a decision only after he had actually seen with his own eyes what the crocodile claimed had happened.

Hunter and crocodile and jackal left the sandbank and moved deep into the bush to where the crocodile had approached the hunter for help.

"Now," said the jackal, "I am prepared to give my verdict. For guiding you home when you were lost the hunter earned your gratitude, but you repaid him by treacherously carrying him to your sandbank where you and your friends were going to eat him. You should be punished for what you did, but I am a compassionate judge so I have decided that you should be left here in the bush to find your own way home again, as if you and the hunter had never met at all."

As the crocodile slithered into the long grass (two days were to pass before he clambered on to his sandbank home, tired and hungry), the jackal said to the hunter, "No, do not thank me, for I have merely repaid a debt. As I said to you yesterday, 'One favour begets another, and as we treat others, so shall we ourselves be treated'."

32

The Man Who Couldn't Keep His Mouth Shut

There may be an imported element in this beautiful story from Equatorial West Africa. The concept of an underground city with gold-paved streets, palaces and a king—a feature of the folklore of Europe and the Middle East—may have been taken over from European and Arab traders who have been active along the Gold Coast for the past four hundred years.

But the legend itself is authentically African.

Mbeku was not a rich man. He was, in fact, rather poor but too proud to admit it. He lived by selling the dates that grew on his palm tree and he was renowned as being the most garrulous man in the neighbourhood. "If you wish to spread a rumour," they used to say, "tell it to Mbeku as a secret, and between the telling and the hearing of it the sun will rise but once."

Now, early one morning, Mbeku climbed the tree, lopped off the cluster of dates in his usual way, fifty bunches that he dropped carefully on to a mat spread out below. When he came down to carry them off to the market, they had disappeared! "There is a thief in our midst," he told all his friends, "and I shall catch him by tomorrow by taking my uncle with me to hide behind a nearby tree and jump out on the thieving rogue."

Early next morning, while he shinned up the tree, his uncle stood guard behind a baobab and watched the fifty clusters dropping one by one on to the mat, but there was no sign of the thief, so he sauntered across to the palm tree and standing right next to the mound of dates shouted up at Mbeku, "No thief today, nephew; we'll have to catch him some other time." But when Mbeku stood at the foot of the tree a moment later, the mat was bare, the dates had disappeared! "This is too much," he said, "much too much. I shall make the long journey to seek advice from Eleri Chia the Wise Priest of the Desert." And this he did on the following day.

When the wise old man had listened silently to

Mbeku's story, never interrupting, just nodding his head sagely from time to time, he said very slowly in his voice cracked with age: "Take this egg, my son, and throw it upon the very spot where the mat lay when the date clusters were piled upon it. But do not speak of this matter to anybody. Remain as silent as the thief himself."

Tired after his long journey, Mbeku slept late, and when the sun was high he stood beneath the tree and hurled the egg at the ground. Splash! He jumped back as a door opened in the ground to reveal many steps leading far down beneath the earth. Slowly he walked down the steps until the doorway above him in the dark seemed no bigger than the sharp-pointed tip of an assegai. Another door opened before him and he was walking along a street made of gold, with houses of silver inlaid with rubies, and everything sparkling and glittering. At the end of the golden street a huge door of silver with golden handles opened silently and he saw before him the hundred clusters of dates stolen from him by the mysterious thief spread out on a mat near a throne made of gold and silver and every precious metal one could imagine—rubies, amethysts, emeralds, and diamonds as large as a grown man's clenched fist.

When he looked up from the mat the throne was occupied by the King of the Ghosts himself, the Lord of the Underworld, resplendent in robes of scarlet and purple. "I have been expecting you,

35

Mbeku," the monarch said, his voice booming and echoing in the vast hall, "ever since I learned that my wicked son had twice stolen your fruit and that the Priest of the Desert had given you an egg. Well, my son is being punished, and when you return to your tree you will find these dates back on the branches again, ready to be plucked and sold in the market."

Mbeku thanked him and turned to go, but the King spoke again: "To make amends for my son's misdemeanours I present you with this magic wand. Whatever you demand of it in the way of worldly goods it shall give to you. But you must not tell anybody of this, for if you do the magic will disappear and misery will stand in its place. Go well, Mbeku, and flourish in silence."

Much later Mbeku stood under his tree again and watched the door closing and being swallowed up by the desert sand. He looked up. Yes, the clusters of dates were back on the tree. Sitting on the ground as the sun shone weakly in the west at the end of the day, he decided what he wanted and asked the wand to get it for him. . . .

Next day the village was buzzing with the story. "Mbeku has a fine house . . . and beautiful wives, fourteen of them and each one more lovely than the next . . . a herd of a thousand cattle, and untold numbers of goats and sheep . . . and more gold and silver than he has dates on his tree . . . Yes, but how? How? He will not speak of it, he who used to talk so much and spill every secret . . . Yes, his silence too is a miracle!"

Mbeku wanted to tell everybody but whenever he was about to do so he heard again in his mind the words of the King of the Ghosts: "But you must not tell anybody of this, for if you do the magic will disappear and misery will stand in its place. Go well, Mbeku, and flourish in silence." For a whole year he was a King among men, and after a time his neighbours stopped asking him how it had happened, but the long silence was so much against his nature that many a night he paced up and down the reception hall in his palatial home, talking to himself, but wanting to talk to the whole world about how good fortune had come to him in the underground kingdom of the King of the Ghosts.

The day came when he could keep his secret to himself no longer. He called his neighbours to assemble in his reception hall where he told them the whole amazing story. No sooner had he finished than the gentle evening exploded into the most savage storm ever known in that part of the world before or since.

The wind was a scream in the night, the sky a river of rain, the earth quaked with the thunder, and the lightning flashes revealed mansion and wives and cattle and everything breaking up and being sucked into the air by the storm. Mbeku's neighbours fought their way back to the village, suddenly emerging as if through a door into the calm of the night while

37

behind them the storm continued to rage until every particle of Mbeku's wealth had disintegrated.

In the morning they found him sitting under his palm tree surrounded by the sand of the desert, with nothing remaining of mansion and wives and cattle and silver and gold and jewels. Mbeku ended his days in poverty and has passed into the realms of legend as "the man who could not keep his mouth shut".

38

The Snake with Five Heads

A Xosa tribesman on the eastern border of the Cape Colony told this story to G. M. Theal the historian in 1882. The Xosas belong to the Bantu-speaking people who are found throughout Africa, from the Cameroons down to the Cape Province and across to South-west Africa.

In THE SNAKE WITH FIVE HEADS, Mpunzikazi meets with disaster because she makes her own marriage arrangements instead of leaving them, as tradition dictates, in the hands of her father or guardian.

After visiting the tribe far across the other side of the river, a chief came back to tell his two daughters

39

that a chief in those parts was seeking a wife. Mpunzikazi the elder daughter, a fiercely proud and arrogant creature, said that she would like to be the one.

"Good, my daughter, I shall call together a large group of warriors to accompany you in the way that is traditional to our people."

"Father, either I go alone or I do not go at all!"

"But that is impossible, my child. A girl going off to meet her husband-to-be in another village must always present herself in a crowd of her own people."

"Father, my mind is made up. I have spoken," said Mpunzikazi, and on the following day she left the village, crossed the river and the plain and was soon swallowed up by the surrounding hills. Soon she met a mouse who kindly offered to show her the way to the chief's abode but she told him rudely to get out of her way or be trodden on. Then she came upon a frog who croaked out his offer of help but she spurned him too, saying that a chief's daughter could not demean herself by conversing with a frog. "Be it on your head," the frog replied before he plopped into a nearby pool.

As the day lengthened she grew tired but kept on walking steadily until she came into a clearing where a herd of goats cropped the grass while the young herdsman, no more than a boy, lay sprawled in the shade of a solitary tree. He rose to his feet as she approached, asking politely, "Where are you going, my sister?"

"You dare to say 'sister' to the daughter of a chief? Out of my way, uncouth ruffian!"

"I am hungry, and beg you to share your bundle of food with me, even if you will not tell me where you are going."

"My business and my food are my own. Go!"

"Sister, take a warning. If you continue in this manner, you will not come back along this road."

But she paid no heed, striding on and then resting in the shade of a huge rock. Out of nowhere an old woman, bent and wrinkled, appeared and stood quavering before her: "My child, along the way the trees will bend their heads and laugh at you, but you must not laugh back at them. And when you find a goatskin bag of milk on a tree-stump you must not drink it. And on no account must you accept a drink of water from a man you will meet who carries his head under his arm. Heed my advice and all will go well with you. Disobey me and you will not pass this way again."

Rested now, Mpunzikazi rose to her feet and shouted at the old woman, "Miserable crone, ancient hag, old and ugly, how dare you tell a chief's daughter what she may and may not do? Out of my way before I push you over!" And she walked into the forest.

As the old woman had foretold, the trees leaned over and roared with laughter. Even the weeping willow chuckled. The chorus of laughter ceased abruptly as Mpunzikazi laughed mockingly at the trees, and all was silent again except for the cawing of a solitary blackbird high in the branches of one of the trees. Through the forest and into a clearing she walked. A goatskin bag of milk lay on top of a tree-stump. She drained it to the dregs and went on walking.

Later that afternoon a man with his head under his arm approached her, offering her a drink from his calabash. She accepted it, without a word of thanks, and continued until she came to the bank of a river and saw the village some distance away on the other side. A young girl who was filling a calabash with water looked up as she approached.

"Where are you going, my sister?"

"Do not call me 'sister'. I, who am the daughter of a chief, am to be the wife of a chief and you will be one of my subjects."

"That may be so, but I advise you not to cross this ford. There is another shallow place farther upsteam. Cross the river there, and enter the village from that side." But Mpunzikazi splashed through the ford and walked through the village gates to where a crowd of men and women had gathered.

"Here I am, the wife-to-be of your chief. Where is my future husband?"

An elderly woman stepped forward and spoke on behalf of all the villagers, with an obvious air of authority: "Firstly, in all my years—and I am the oldest here—I have never heard of a girl all on her own coming to seek a husband. Secondly, the chief is away at the moment. Thirdly, he will be hungry when he comes home, so take this grain to his hut, grind it fine and make some bread for his supper." And the villagers nodded their heads in agreement.

"I shall do this," said Mpunzikazi, "but after I have become the wife of your chief you will all of you take your orders from me. You may go now." The villagers went to their huts, some smiling, some laughing broadly. The old woman shook her head sadly and the sun dropped down over the horizon.

The girl did not grind the grain finely and she baked so carelessly that the crust was badly burned. As she placed the loaf on the wooden table, a great wind sprang up suddenly and whirled the sand everywhere into dust. The skin covering the entrance to the hut shook as a long thick snake with five heads and big eyes on each came inside, curled up and began to eat the bread. For the first time in her life the girl knew fear. The five heads choked on the bread and growled in angry unison: "We do not like your cooking. We, Makanda Mahluna, do not want you as our bride."

The tail of the snake swung round and struck Mpunzikazi. The girl disappeared and in her place stood a frog that croaked despairingly before hopping out of the hut to plop into the river.

One year later Mpunzikazi's younger sister Mpunzanyana was of marriageable age and told her father that she wanted to cross the river and be a chief's wife. "My daughter, you may go, but only if you are one of many. Your sister went alone and has never been seen again. You must follow our traditions and have a retinue. Many warriors must accompany you on your journey. Go well, my child."

Along the way they met a mouse who offered to show Mpunzanyana the way. She accepted his advice gratefully and graciously, and did the same when a frog wanted to help them. A boy looking after a herd of goats asked her for food and she shared her bundle with him. Then an old woman, bent and wrinkled, appeared before them and quavered to the girl: "Daughter, listen to me and prosper. When the trees of the forest laugh at you, remain silent and do not even smile in return. Do not drink the goatskin bag of milk on a tree-stump and do not accept the offer of a drink of water from a man who carries his head under his arm."

"Mother, you speak and I obey."

"And one more warning. After all I have described to you has happened, you will find yourself having to choose where the road forks. Take the narrow path, for the wide one leads to certain doom."

"I thank you, mother."

She heeded every word of advice; and when the bridal retinue was walking one behind the other along the narrow path, the girl in front, a black-bird flew down out of the tree, alighted on her shoulder and cawed hoarsely in her ear: "The village of the chief is not far from here. An old woman will

44

give you grain to make bread. Grind it fine and do not burn the crust. And no matter what happens, no matter how difficult you find it to understand, do not be afraid, for truly there is nothing to fear and only joy for you." And the blackbird flapped away into the forest.

When they came to the river, she accepted the advice of a girl who was filling a calabash with water and went upstream before splashing through the ford and entering the village, the girl walking in front and behind her all the warriors of her father the chief. A crowd of men and women stood before them and an elderly woman stepped out to ask her what she was doing in those parts.

"I and my people have come a long way and this is the end of my journey. Tomorrow the bridal party will return across the river and I shall stay to become the wife of your chief."

"Will fear possess you when you see your husband-to-be for the first time?"

"No, I shall not be afraid."

"Come, then, take this grain and bake bread so that my son may eat when he comes home. I am the mother of the chief."

Mpunzanyana ground the grain very fine and was careful to make beautiful bread, crusty but not black with careless burning, and when it was done she sat down to rest and await the coming of her future husband while her father's warriors relaxed and ate in the very large hut reserved for visitors.

45

Suddenly the dust was everywhere as the wind sprang up violently. With the hut shaking, and some of the poles supporting it falling about her, the girl sat calmly waiting.

The force of the wind blew away the skin that covered the entrance to the hut and the girl found herself gazing into the big eyes of a snake with five heads. She was afraid, but did not show it and watched the five heads eating the bread she had baked with skill and care. Then all five heads spoke in unison, a chorus of approval: "Your bread is very good. It pleases us greatly. You shall be our bride. Here, these ornaments are our wedding gift to you." And a shower of gold and silver and copper bangles and necklaces and ear-rings fell at the girl's feet.

The chief's mother entered the hut and said, "Let the wedding commence. Let the feasting begin." And at that very moment Makanda Mahluna the snake with five heads vanished and in his place, strong and handsome, stood Makanda Mahluna the young man, the chief who since childhood had been under an evil spell finally broken by the steadfastness of Mpunzanyana.

Chief and mother hugged the girl in gratitude and the villagers stamped and cheered to see their chief return to them as a man—and with such a beautiful and courageous bride.

It was a happy marriage, blessed with many children.

The Girl Who Disobeyed

Nogoma, the heroine of THE GIRL WHO DISOBEYED, has to suffer for disregarding the ritual of Ntongana which requires a girl to stay indoors until she is called to join the celebrations by a son of her father's chief councillor. This story was also collected by G. M. Theal from a Xosa tribesman.

"Every year when the tribe performs the ceremony of Ntongane, tradition compels me as the chief's daughter to remain in my hut while they dance and feast outside," Nogoma was thinking, her feet

47

moving to the rhythm of drum and whistle and pounding dance that reached her ears from the ceremonial ground some distance away. At that moment shrill laughter knocked at the door, and the girls who were her friends were asking her to swim with them in the river that flowed past the kraal, even though they all knew it was against the rules of the tribe of Ntongane. Because she was wilful, Nogoma joined them.

Leaving their clothes and beads and bangles on the riverbank, they dived into the water, splashing and laughing, the sounds of the ceremony a mere whisper in their ears. Then one girl shrieked and pointed towards the bank. A big white snake with black stripes called Isinyolo was lifting its head above its coils as if guarding the pile of clothes, and the girls were very frightened, with the exception of one of them who swam towards the snake, then stood up in the water and sang:

> "Isinyolo, snake of fame,
> Isinyolo of many powers,
> Let me have my mantle back,
> The black one with the golden flowers."

Its head swaying rhythmically, the snake hissed in reply:

> "Take your clothes, take them away,
> But do not swim on such a day.
> Ntongane you must obey.
> Nogoma in her hut should stay
> Instead of coming out to play."

48

One by one the four girls sang to Isinyolo, and each time he hissed his refrain before letting them approach him and collect their possessions. But Nogoma was proud, as befits a chief's daughter, and irritable, because she knew she had done wrong by not obeying the tradition, so, instead of pleading as the others had done, she shouted: "I am the chief's daughter who begs no favours. I am coming out of the water to collect my clothes and Isinyolo can go back to wherever he belongs!" Hissing in his anger, the snake bit her as she walked towards him, and her friends were so horrified when she changed colour, white with black stripes just like Isinyolo, that they fled back to the kraal and did not say a word to anybody about the swimming, the snake, or how Nogoma had changed colour. Even when the chief sent search parties into every corner of his territory to seek his lost daughter, the four girls said nothing.

Nogoma, shocked to find herself striped, and ashamed of what she had done on the day of Ntongane, had run into the forest and hidden herself in a tree, sustaining herself with berries and nuts that she picked from bushes every morning. On the fourth day she looked down to see a young hunter, walking into the clearing, and he looked up bemused, thinking he heard a voice saying, "Tell the chief on this side of the river that his daughter Nogoma was bitten by Isinyolo and is now white with black stripes, ashamed to be seen." He shook

49

his head disbelievingly and was about to go when he heard the voice again, more tearful and insistent than before, and looking up into the branches he could see Nogoma. He ran off to deliver her message to her father.

That afternoon the chief and his two sons called Nogoma down from the tree, horrified to see how she had changed and furious at her disobedience on the day of Ntongane. "Your brothers will bring you home after darkness falls so that nobody can look upon you," he said, "and I shall have to follow the tribal custom that will send you far away, with forty men and a herd of cattle so that evil will not flow from you to the rest of our tribe." And that very night Nogoma and forty young men left their village with a herd of cattle.

Many miles from where Isinyolo had struck, they built two huts for themselves and a big barn for the cattle; and Nogoma gave orders for the cows to be milked. Nobody could stop the flood of milk, which flowed along a ditch into a mighty hole in the ground which soon filled up right to the brim while the milk kept pouring in. But instead of overflowing it rose and rose until a huge white mound of milk cast a shadow over the huts in the new settlement.

By this time pandemonium had brought Nogoma out of her hut, and she heard a deep voice from within the white mountain of milk calling her to approach. All the young men stood far back as the girl walked proudly to the column of milk. As she touched it they saw it become liquid again and engulf the chief's daughter. Then the milk was gone and the ground hard and dry and Nogoma stood smiling and beautiful, the stripes gone, her body as brown as on the day of Ntongane before Isinyolo had bitten her on the bank of the river. "Now we can all go back to our home village," was the thought in every man's mind, and Nogoma spoke their thoughts aloud but added, "First we shall send a messenger to our chief my father tomorrow to tell him what has happened."

But before the messenger could leave, a young chief walked into the encampment and when he saw Nogoma his heart turned over and he said, "Beautiful maiden, I am a chief's son and my father insists that I can marry nobody but a chief's daughter. But you are so lovely that I want you for my wife, and if you are willing I shall tell my father so."

"I am willing," Nogoma said quietly, "for you please me greatly. And my father the chief will be glad to hear of it."

So they married; and since that time Isinyolo has never appeared on the bank of the river again.

The Glutton

This story is very well known in Southern Africa among the tribes making up the Bantu—Zulu, Xosa, Basuto, Bechuana, Shangaan, Herero.

Highly imaginative, it makes its moral point without becoming didactic.

Sebgugugu was a very poor man, with a wife and three little children, his only possessions a white cow and a calf, so there was milk for the family. But his plot of land was stony and did not yield very

much. So he listened intently when a bird alighted
on the back of the white cow and sang to him:

> "I'll promise you a hundred more
> Standing lowing at your door
> If you'll kill the white cow—
> Now!"

That night he discussed this strange happening
with his wife who said he must have been dreaming
and in any case what would they do for milk if he
killed the cow? But on the next day the bird came
down again and sang from the back of the white
cow:

> "Kill the white cow, kill!
> And your fields I will fill
> With a hundred cows.
> A hundred for one!
> Will it be done?"

This time Sebgugugu did not discuss the matter
with his wife but took an axe and slaughtered the
animal, and all through that week his wife was
saying over and over, "We have beef to eat but the
cow is gone and where are the hundred cows the
magic bird promised you in your dreams?"

Less than a week went by before the bird came
down again, and standing on the back of the calf it
sang this song:

> "You've killed the cow,
> Now kill the calf,

And when you do
One hundred cows
Will come to you."

Even as the bird was flying away, Sebgugugu took his axe and slaughtered the calf, saying to himself, "This is no time for half-measures. There is too much at stake." Every morning he awoke early, listening eagerly for the lowing of one hundred cattle and the sound of their hooves on his stony patch of ground. Then he would get up and look, to see only the arid soil, the one dried-up tree, and far away the hills, but not a single cow. Every day his wife cursed him for a fool, and when they had no meat left they had to set out to seek food, for Sebgugugu, his wife, and their three little children.

Along the way they met an old man resting in the shade of a tree. He recognised them at once. "Sebgugugu," he said, "I have been waiting for you. The bird told me to expect you and your family. Now listen carefully to what I have to say: Not far from here you will find a kraal. Enter, drink the calabash of cow's milk, and when the cattle come home you must give their herdsman milk to drink, but you must never abuse or strike him. Kraal and cattle are yours."

"Is the herdsman man or boy and is he one of our tribe?"

"He is neither man nor boy, nor is he one of your tribe. The herdsman is a white-necked crow who

54

must always be treated as you would treat your own family. Go well, Sebgugugu, and prosper."

He did as the old man had said, and that evening the cattle came home, herded by a white-necked crow who flew up and down, back and forth, making sure that none of the animals strayed. Sebgugugu gave the bird milk and counted the cattle. They totalled exactly one hundred. The years went by and the children grew, and one night Sebgugugu said to his wife: "I am getting tired of feeding the white-necked crow. The children are old enough to herd our cattle now. I shall kill that bird tomorrow."

When his wife pleaded with him, he replied that it had been his decision to kill the cow and calf that had brought them a kraal and a hundred cattle, and he had decided to kill the white-necked crow. Next evening, when the bird herded the cattle home, Sebgugugu gave it milk and while it was drinking he returned to his house, taking down his bow and an arrow, and aiming through the doorway. The bow vibrated in his hand, the arrow sped towards the bird but, without even looking at him, it flew into the air and as the arrow hit the log it had just vacated, the cattle disappeared and Sebgugugu gazed out upon an empty kraal.

Once again the family had to tramp the roads in search of food, and once again they met the old man sitting in the shade of a tree. "Sebgugugu," he said, "the bird has told me of your doing, and although you do not deserve a second chance I will give it to you. Pay strict attention to what I tell you now: Across the field, past that distant baobab tree, you will come upon a melon-vine in the bush, and upon it many different fruits and vegetables are growing. Eat your fill every day, but on no account must you water the vine or prune it. Go well, Sebgugugu, and prosper."

And prosper he did, he and his family, for many months, living in the kraal and collecting their food from the melon-vine, until the day that Sebgugugu made the decision—in spite of his wife's protests—to prune the vine and make it yield even more. One snip was all it took to make the vine shrivel, wither, and disappear. Hungry once again, he and his family tramped the road in search of food.

This time the old man sitting in the shade of the tree was less cordial than he had been on the previous occasions. "Sebgugugu," he said, "you are a glutton. Even when you are wallowing in abundance, you want more. Twice this greed has caused your downfall; you are not deserving of another chance, but I shall give you one more, your very last. Fail again and you fail for ever."

"Old man," he replied, "I know I have been foolish, but adversity has taught me a hard lesson. One more chance is all I need to redeem myself and to keep starvation away from my wife and children."

"Listen most carefully, then," the old man said. "Outside your kraal, on your return, you will find a rock with small cracks in it out of which will come pouring corn, milk, meat, and a variety of fruits and vegetables, three times every day. This rock will go on providing for you and your family far into the future, even when you are as old as I am now, but you must not tamper with the rock in any way. Just leave it to do its work of providing for you. Go well, Sebgugugu, and keep a firm check on your gluttony."

It was as the old man had said, and the years went by idyllically for Sebgugugu and his family, until his own greed overpowered him again. Sitting watching the food pouring steadily from the cracks one morning, he said to himself, "If I can widen the cracks in this rock, perhaps it will pour out food not three times a day but all through the day and the night. Not only will I have more to eat myself, but there will be a great surplus for selling in the market. I will be rich!"

That night he did not discuss his decision with his wife. He knew what *her* attitude would be! Next morning, while the others were still asleep, he collected a long thick pole from the kraal and walked down to the rock which had started to pour food as soon as the first rays of the morning sun touched its side. Sebgugugu sharpened one end of the pole and when the food stopped flowing he plunged it into one of the cracks. Without a sound the cracks closed up one by one, then the rock itself vanished, and Sebgugugu stood there with the pole in his hand.

57

Slowly he walked back to the kraal, fearing the righteous wrath of his wife. But where kraal and wife and three sons had been, there was nothing, only the hard stony ground. He ran down the road to seek the old man resting in the shade of the tree. But there was no old man, not even a tree.

He stood there in utter desolation. Looking up, he saw a white-necked crow circling slowly above him. Then it flew away and he stared after it until it was a dot in the sky. Then it was gone and Sebgugugu began to walk down the long road.

The Boy on the Ox's Back

The saga of Kamaga and his white ox Ubongopa is a Zulu
nursery tale, first recorded in Natal by the Rev. Canon
Callaway, M.D., in the middle of the nineteenth century.

The Zulus, fierce warriors whose leaders included the great
chiefs Chaka and Cetshwayo, were defeated by the British
Army at the Battle of Isandhlwana, Natal, in 1879.

They form part of the widespread Bantu tribes.

Shortly before the chief's wife gave birth to a son, an
ox was born, so perfectly formed, so regal, that the
chief said, "When our child comes into the world I

59

shall place him on the white ox's back. I shall call
the animal Ubongopa." After the child, named
Kamaga, had come into the world, he was placed
on the ox's back where he stayed day and night,
eating his food, growing, scorning a blanket on the
coldest night when water became ice, and guarding
the kraal of his father.

Every morning he said to the white ox:

> "Awake, Ubongopa,
> Awake and arise,
> For the sun comes up
> In the morning skies."

And when the ox rose to its feet, the boy still on
its back, Kamaga would say:

> "Let us set out,
> It is time to go.
> Tell all the cattle
> So they will know
> That the day is new
> And the grass is sweet
> With morning dew."

Ubongopa would bellow, the cattle would get up
on sleep-wobbly feet, bellowing to wake the kraal,
and the long line of cattle would move out into the
pastureland to graze and wander. Late in the afternoon Kamaga would say:

> "Return to the kraal
> The sun is sinking
> Soon the leopard will be slinking

> Eager for battle
> Hungry for cattle
> Through the tall grass silently creeping
> Come! It is time for dreaming and sleeping."

And when they entered the kraal as the sun went to sleep, pulling its vast red blanket over the horizon, and the gates of the kraal closed behind the straggling herd, Kamaga would eat his supper on Ubongopa's back, and with the first stars suddenly twinkling in the sky he would say:

> "Sleep now, my cattle,
> Sleep till the morn
> When the crow of the rooster
> Wakens the dawn.
> Cold in the night the dew is falling,
> Tomorrow the sweet grass will be calling."

So he grew into young manhood with the passing years.

One night, when the moon was down and the night was black, thieves from a neighbouring tribe stole into the kraal and tried to drive the cattle out into the bush by beating them with sticks. But the sticks broke, each one of them, and the cattle didn't even stir from their sleep. Four times the thieves were confounded by their sticks breaking, and on the fifth night they beat the cattle with bundles of sticks but these too splintered and broke off in their hands. On the sixth night they tried once more, with the same result, but each man kept one stick intact, and Kamaga heard their leader whisper, "There, sitting on that white ox, is the cause of our sticks breaking every night," and coming up to Kamaga he said, "Tell the cattle to move or you will die on that ox of yours." And Kamaga spoke very softly:

> "Let us set out.
> It is time to go.
> Tell all the cattle
> So they will know
> That the day is new
> And the grass is sweet
> With morning dew.
> We're going where we've never been,
> Captured by thieves we've never seen."

Ubongopa lowed urgently and quietly in the dark, and the cattle moved slowly through the open gate and were gone. The leader of the thieves growled at Kamaga: "You come too, you on your fine white ox, or my men will kill you." The young man replied calmly:

> "No one can stab me; I cannot die.
> Stab me and break your sharp assegai.
> But I'll come with you, no matter how far,
> And with me my mighty ox Ubongopa.
> We're going where we've never been,
> Captured by thieves we've never seen."

When morning came, Kamaga and Ubongopa

and the cattle gone, the wise man of the tribe said to the chief, "Your son the king to be is now a man, for he has spirited the cattle away while his people were sleeping, thus fulfilling the traditions of our tribe. Food must be prepared, and beer brewed. This is a time of rejoicing for our tribe." And they caroused, but when darkness came again the people wondered what had happened to Kamaga. . .

He had been taken to the chief of the neighbouring tribe who was addressed by the leader of the thieves: "We have lost many nights trying to steal the cattle whose backs broke our sticks but who felt no pain from the blows because they have been bewitched by the one who is called Kamaga and who sits on the white ox Ubongopa which is the source of his magic power. Kill the ox and its master's power will drain away with its blood."

"We will make him come down to the ground," the chief said, ordering Kamaga to lead the cattle into an enclosure, which he did by saying:

"Ubongopa, lead the cattle away
To where the chief says they must stay.
We're going where we've never been,
Captured by thieves we've never seen."

Then the chief commanded the young man to come down to the ground, but he replied, "I live up here, you live down there. My feet have never touched the ground." Again the chief ordered him to dismount and this time he said:

63

"Ubongopa, I am getting down
To walk upon the ground, the earth,
Having lived upon your sturdy back
Ever since the day of my birth.
We're going to where we've never been,
Captured by thieves we've never seen."

They took him to a tumbledown house with holes
in the roof through which he could see the stars, and
when they brought him food he cried: "Take it
away, for I cannot eat my food on the ground, only
on the back of my white ox Ubongopa." And he
spat upon the ground in his disgust, and the people
fled into the nearby hills, taking all their cattle with
them, for the spittle grew and grew while a voice
from within was heard to say in booming tones:

"You are as great as yonder mountain,
Making a heap of spittle a fountain,
To make the clouds pour out their rain
With thunder and lightning again and again!"

The sky turned black, the rain came down like a
river, but only on the village, nowhere else, and
when the people on the hilltop saw this every time
the lightning lit the scene, the thunder shaking the
earth, they believed that Kamaga must be drowned
and with him all his cattle, for nobody could survive
such a deluge. Then the sunshine came again and
they returned to their village where the water was
still pouring out of their houses. But as dry as the
sands of the desert in summer the young man sat in

front of the ramshackle house, the only dwelling not affected by the storm. Kamaga's cattle stood placidly by as if nothing untoward had happened.

"You see," cried the leader of the thieves, "there is magic in him. It comes from the white ox. Kill the ox and we destroy the young man's power."

The chief ordered the ox to be slaughtered; the leader of the thieves stabbed at Ubongopa with his assegai and the villagers gasped as the spear bounced off the ox's hide and stabbed him in the arm, drawing blood. The chief turned on Kamaga. "Tell the white ox it must die, or you will be killed yourself." And the young man said soothingly:

"Ubongopa, it is time to die,
As swiftly as the falling rain.
But you will feel no pain, no pain,
And one day we shall meet again.
We're going where we've never been,
Captured by thieves we've never seen."

They killed the ox, skinned it and cut it into many pieces. A fire was made and the chief announced that the white ox would be eaten. "But before we roast the meat let us all go down to the river to bathe our bodies so that any evil spirits will be washed away." While they were gone, Kamaga placed all the portions of meat on the spread-out ox-skin and standing over it spoke these words:

"Awake, Ubongopa,
Awake and arise,

65

> For the sun comes up
> In the morning skies."

As the ox stood up Kamaga said:

> "Let us set out,
> It is time to go
> Into the hills
> And the valleys below
> Where the grass is sweet
> With morning dew."

With Kamaga on his back and the cattle moving into line behind them, they passed through the gate only to be met by the villagers whose chief cried out, "Kill the boy, kill him, my warriors!" And Kamaga spoke again:

> "Ubongopa, stop! We must not run.
> The time for fighting has begun.
> This is the hour of the assegai—
> But who will live and who will die?"

When the chief ordered him to dismount from the white ox's back he did so and walked unafraid towards the warriors. "Kill!" cried the chief, and the warriors hurled their assegais which arched through the air and then stuck in the ground in front of Kamaga. The warriors, frightened now, pulled them out and flung them a second time. Again they stuck quivering in the earth, and this time all the men fell back in awe.

"Now you will all die," said Kamaga, plucking

66

one of the assegais out of the ground and throwing it with all his force at the chief who dropped down dead and with him all the villagers. Then the young man tapped the chief's body with the haft of an assegai and he and all his people stood upright again, all afraid with the exception of the chief who grabbed an assegai and lifted it to throw. But Kamaga spat on the ground and the spittle grew into a barrier in which the chief's assegai stuck while a voice boomed inside:

"You are as great as yonder mountain,
Great as the peaks that reach to the sun.
Throw your spear at the savage chieftain—
Do to him what he has done."

A spear whistled through the air, the chief fell and all the people with him, lying motionless on the ground. With the haft of an assegai, Kamaga tapped them one by one, and one after another they rose from the ground to stand upright, all except the chief who lay where he had fallen. Surrounding Kamaga, they chanted in unison:

"You are our leader,
We are your people,
Yours to command,
Ours to obey
From this moment,
From today!"

With the passing of many days in many places,

the action repeated itself until Kamaga was at the head of three tribes, with all their cattle added to his, and he always sitting on Ubongopa's back. Then he sent a messenger to tell his father that he was alive and would be coming home. But his father would not believe it until Kamaga sent him an ox that he knew had been in the kraal the night that his son had disappeared. This is the message he sent to his son: "Come home, my son, your people await you, to be their leader when I have gone. And I have chosen a beautiful bride for you— the daugher of Ubingani who is the son of the mighty Umakula."

Soon after that they saw Kamaga riding on his white ox and behind him the people of the three tribes and all their cattle and they heard him singing again:

"Return to the kraal,
The sun is sinking,
Soon the leopard will be slinking:
Eager for battle,
Hungry for cattle,
Through the tall grass silently creeping.
Come! It is time for dreaming and sleeping."

His father embraced him, there was feasting with dancing and singing far into the night, but no marriage, because Kamaga said that he could not marry anybody who lived on the ground as it was his destiny to live on the back of Ubongopa until his life came to an end. He lived for many years, and his magic powers made his life a saga.

Today, hundreds of years afterwards, he is a legend in that part of Africa where the herders still say to their cattle when the first stars suddenly twinkle in the sky the words that Kamaga had used in the long ago:

"Sleep now, my cattle,
Sleep till the morn
When the crow of the rooster
Wakens the dawn.
Cold in the night the dew is falling.
Tomorrow the sweet grass will be calling."

Reaching for the Sun

H. Chatelein heard this beautiful story from a Bantu-speaking tribe in Angola late in the nineteenth century. It incorporates a Jacob's Ladder in the form of a spider's web, which is found in the folklore of the Angola Bantu and the Hausas of the Sudan.

The personification of the moon as the sun's wife is very interesting, for among the Bantu in general the moon is masculine and has two wives—the Evening Star and the Morning Star.

"Kimanuele, now that you are a man it is time to think of getting married," said the chief of a great tribe to his son one morning. "Whom do you wish to be your bride? Choose well, my son, for one day you will take my place as chief and she will be the mother of the child that will become chief after you."

"Father," replied Kimanuele, "I have already made up my mind. Not one young maiden that I have seen upon the earth pleases me. I wish to marry the daughter of the Sun and Moon!" When the chief realised after much discussion that his son's mind could not be changed, he told him to write a letter to Lord Sun and Lady Moon, but who could deliver it for him?

He asked the deer, antelope, hawk and vulture, but each animal and bird shook its head, saying, No, such a mission could not be accomplished. Then Minuti the frog was ushered into the chief's presence, bulging eyes blinking, throat throbbing. "Great chief," he croaked, "the wind has whispered to the reeds and the reeds have confided in the water that you need a messenger to take a letter to Lord Sun and Lady Moon. Let me serve you, chief, for truly there is a way and I alone know it." And armed with the letter, and the chief's gratitude, he hopped away to a well so concealed with rushes that he alone in the whole kingdom had drunk of its water.

As night dropped down over the world, a cord spun by untold numbers of golden spiders came down out of the sky and holding on to it were two shining maidens, gold in front and silver at the back, carrying big jugs. Because the frog had watched them before, hidden in his well, his croaking silenced by their gleaming beauty, he knew that they were the servants of Lord Sun and Lady Moon and that they came down to the earth to collect water, because there was no moisture on the sun.

The frog slipped silently into one of the jugs, the water bubbling and splashing with the scooping, and in the darkness could feel the bobbing as the rope was pulled up into the starry night. Much later he awoke from a long sleep when the jug bumped to rest on a table. Hopping out, he leaned the chief's letter against one of the jugs and hid himself in a corner black with darkness.

Scintillating, blazing, shining, Lord Sun flowed into the room. "However did this letter reach me from the world below?" he cried out before reading it aloud: "I, Kimanuele, son of Africa's most majestic chief, wish to marry the daughter of Lord Sun and Lady Moon." Lord Sun laughed. "Impudent fellow! But one must admire his initiative and praise his ingenuity for he lives down there and I rule up here, yet his letter has reached me. I wonder how he did it?" He crumpled the letter and threw it burning into a corner of the room.

Then the stars faded and through the window the frog could see the sunshine illuminating the faraway earth. Again he slept, and when he awoke the stars were bright in the blackness of the night and the beautiful gold-and-silver maidens were getting ready to fetch water again. Hopping noiselessly into an empty jug, he slept again, waking to the creaking croak of a sleeping bullfrog, the pattering scurry of ants on guard outside their heap, and a sleepless cricket seeking sympathy with the sad monotony of his music. Just as the water began to pour in, he leaped out of the jug and at the rising of the sun he was standing before Kimanuele's father saying, "Mighty chief, I have delivered your son's letter to Lord Sun who was impressed by its reaching him and mystified by how it got there, but has made no reply. May I venture to suggest that you ask your son to write again in six days from now when I shall return to you?"

This the chief did, giving Minuti the frog a letter which went as follows: "Lord and Lady Sun, I wrote to you saying that I would marry your daughter. I know my letter was delivered, for my messenger saw you reading it, but there has been no reply to tell me what your answer is, so my messenger will come again a second time."

Once again the frog was lifted into the heavens in a jug of water, and this time, from his hiding-place in the same dark corner as before, he watched Lord Sun writing a letter and propping it against one of the jugs. Back to earth he went on the following night and on the next morning he gave the letter to the chief who read it with obvious delight. "I am so impressed by your ingenuity and persistence that I

73

agree to you and my daughter marrying, but I shall be even more impressed when the first instalment of the dowry for her is a golden heap on my table."

On his next ascent into the heavens Minuti carried a letter and a small bag of gold. "Look, my dears," said Lord Sun to Lady Moon and their daughter—a shimmering beauty—on the following day. "Here is gold, and a letter that says, 'Lord Sun, I show you the first part of the dowry. The remainder I shall send you when you let me know what it shall be.'" Because he was in no hurry to see his daughter married and gone for ever from his kingdom, he cried out, "Who is this mysterious one who delivers letters and gold from my daughter's suitor on the earth, bringing them up through the vast heavens far far higher than even eagles have ventured? After such a journey he is surely ravenously hungry. Roast a chicken for him to eat tonight!" And when Lord Sun came to write his reply next morning, only the bones lay in the bowl on the table.

That night the frog stood upon the earth again, watching the gold-and-silver maidens carrying their jugs of water and sliding up the sky to where the sun was sleeping and invisible from our world. Next morning the chief read the letter: "Kimanuele, chief's son, your first present has been delivered. The remainder shall be a sack filled with gold."

Three days went by before the sack was filled with the precious gold-dust and the frog was able to place it on Lord Sun's table together with a letter from Kimanuele which proclaimed: "Here is the dowry. Soon I myself shall scale the heavens and bring home my wife your daughter."

"Roast a hog for the mysterious messenger to eat tonight!" roared Lord Sun. And in the morning, after his servants had removed the bones from the table, he wrote: "Choose the day on which you will come to heaven to claim your bride who awaits her husband." Down the night the frog rode, inside an empty jug at the end of a rope spun by a multitude of spiders, to stand before the chief and his son at the next rising of the sun. Kimanuele was sad. "We've gone so far but we can go no farther. I have consulted many wise men while you have been away but nobody can help the son of their chief to fly into the heavens to reach Lord Sun and bring home his bride. Minuti, audacious and heroic frog, you have achieved so much on my behalf already. How much more can we expect of you?"

That night, when the gold-and-silver maidens carried the jugs of water from the well to Lord Sun's table, the frog rode with them, awake this time for he was working out a plan of action. As they placed the jugs on the table he hopped into the corner that had served him before as a hiding-place and waited until the maidens who had carried him up from the world had gone yawning out of the room.

Along the corridor and into the bedroom of Lord

75

Sun's daughter he plopped, to gaze upon the sleep-ing girl who was radiantly beautiful. From the incredibly tiny calabash he carried he poured a few drops of liquid upon her eyelids before hiding him-self in a corner of the room and sleeping soundly until frightened cries awoke him. Lord Sun's daughter, groping, her hands stretched out before her, was blundering into the furniture while trying to reach the door.

The frog was not surprised, knowing that the liquid he had poured on to her eyelids had made her blind. Lord Sun and Lady Moon rushed into the room. "I cannot see!" moaned their daughter. "I am blind!"

Lord Sun called for Ngombo, very old and wizened, a man who was wise in addition to being a doctor, and after he had examined the girl's eyes he quavered, "I believe that a spell has been placed upon your daughter, and I would say that her lover on the earth is responsible. Why? Because he is unable to come up here, he is making it necessary for her to go down there. I am sure that he will be able to cure her, for is he not powerful enough to have placed a spell upon her from far, far away across the immensity of the heavens?" The girl's parents could only agree with his diagnosis.

Lord Sun then ordered the limitless hordes of golden spiders to spin a web long enough to reach the earth, strong enough to bear the weight of his daughter and her attendants, and ornamental enough to reflect the power and culture and feeling for beauty of the Sun family.

While the spiders were industriously spinning and weaving, the frog returned to the well with the gold-and-silver girls, and after watching them ascending into the heavens he was lulled to sleep by the rhythmically marching feet of the centipede, the black beetle with the brown spot that taps on the ground and is called Tok-Tokkie, and the distant chiming of the blades of grass made to bump into one another by a delicate breeze.

The birds had whistled the dawn into the sky when Minuti told Kimanuele and his father the chief that in six days' time he would bring Lord Sun's daughter to them. "That will be time enough for preparations for the wedding ceremony."

Five nights from that day the spider web was completed. Guided by the gold-and-silver girls, sad at leaving the sun her home but joyous at the prospect of meeting Kimanuele her lover, the blinded daughter of Lord Sun and Lady Moon came down to the earth. They left her standing at the well and were tugged back into the sky at the end of the intricate spider-web, which later that night became entangled with some stars and stayed in the sky forever, to be called by man The Milky Way.

The girl waited patiently until the frog restored her sight with a tiny purple berry whose juice he squeezed on to her eyelids. Her first view of the earth was sunrise red in the east, tipping the hilltops with fire, the flaming hibiscus, the pink-and-white mimosa, and a thousand swallows swarming singing overhead as if they were lifting the sun into the African sky. She was enchanted by such beauty, and clapped her hands together in delight as Minuti the frog told her the full story behind her coming to live on the earth.

Her first celebration on the earth was her own wedding, so vast and sumptuous that the story-tellers still describe it in meticulous detail in that part of Africa. She and Kimanuele loved each other mightily, lived long and happily, and had many children. Minuti the frog declined all the rewards and honours that were offered him, and because of what he accomplished the frogs in that part of Africa are regarded to this day as being very wise—wiser even than the tortoise, which is the greatest compliment of all.

The Onion-Seekers

Here is a Bantu story that is known in various parts of Africa, and in the south among the Zulu, Xosa and Basuto tribes. Escaping from ogres is the theme of many Bantu stories, and there is a multitude of variants. In some cases the giant is turned into a tree which takes over his harmful powers, becoming, for example, a home for the fiercest and most dangerous bee-hive in all Africa.

Two girls set out to dig for onions where they grew some distance from their village across the plain.

While they were filling their sacks a big one-eyed man about four times as high as themselves sauntered out of the forest and came up to them. He seemed kindly enough, despite his size, and they conversed with him without fear. "Come back to this same place tomorrow," he said, "and I'll show you the patch where the best and biggest onions grow."

On the following day he showed them the place and as they started digging the elder sister realised that the area was covered with a multitude of outsize footprints. "Many people have been here recently," she said. "Are you not alone?"

"I have been walking about a great deal," he replied, "up and down, round and about, seeking this patch for you." But the girl felt uneasy because the footprints deeply implanted in the earth were not all the same size, so without saying a word she glanced discreetly in various directions while digging for the onions.

"What a strange girl you are," laughed One-Eye, "always stopping to look and listen while your sister digs up two onions to every one of yours." And then she saw it! Looking into a hole dug by an anteater, she glimpsed some men who did not see her because she was looking down on the tops of their heads. So she was not surprised when One-Eye called to them across the patch to attract their attention while his friends came up out of the anteater's hole and then strolled across to them as if they had walked casually out of the forest.

The elder sister heard One-Eye whispering that these girls were the two succulent morsels he had told them about the day before, and she began to plan their escape even as One-Eye struck up a sprightly tune on a flute made from a reed and the big men asked the two girls to join them in a dance.

As they danced in a big circle, their heads reaching up to the giants' knees, the elder sister tied the end of her cloak to her sister's, and with the giants singing and shuffling, their shadows moving crazily on the ground, she whispered to her sister, "When I tug your cloak, follow me, but walk backwards and step into my footprints, otherwise these giants will have us for their supper."

When the giants began to concentrate on the dance-steps that grew more and more difficult as One-Eye played increasingly intricate melodies on his reed, the two girls slipped away, walking backwards rapidly until they were able to scramble into the hole made by the ant-eater. There they sat, scarcely daring to breathe while the ground shook with the dancing feet.

Suddenly they heard One-Eye's voice. "Where are the dancing girls?" and voices replied, "You cannot see them with only one eye, One-Eye. Play on!" But the music didn't start up again, the dancing stopped, the ground trembled no longer, and they could hear voices saying, "They have disappeared! But how? There's only one set of tiny footprints on the ground, and they lead to us and not away from us." The earth shook again as the giants rushed pounding from one part of the onion patch to another seeking the two girls who had disappeared so mysteriously—and so inconveniently, just before suppertime! "Let us cover ourselves with cobwebs to make their seeing us more difficult," whispered the elder sister.

A moment later the rumbling grew very loud and the sun was blotted out above them. "There they are!" cried One-Eye, pointing at the ant-eater's hole, but the others laughed and said that if they with their two eyes each couldn't see the girls how could One-Eye expect them to believe that he had spied them.

"All right," they heard a voice saying, "just to make sure, I'll poke my assegai down the hole." And as the tip of the assegai scratched the little girl's arm and drew a trickle of blood, her sister motioned her not to cry out.

"Nobody there, One-Eye," laughed the giants, "but if you can spy them with your little eye, stay here while we go down to the river to drink." The footsteps receded, and a great thud told them that One-Eye was lying down on the ground above them. The elder sister whispered an incantation:

> "In your mouth your tongue is dry,
> You are so thirsty you will die
> Unless you drink down at the river."

They could hear One-Eye walking across the

field and down to the river. They scrambled out of the ant-eater's hole in the ground and ran hand-in-hand across the onion patch and on to the plain that led to their village and safety. When the little girl became so exhausted that she could run no farther, her sister carried her on her back until she too was about to drop from exhaustion. From far away they heard the cry, "There they are, in the distance, on the plain. Catch them before they can reach their village and put the warriors on to us!" Putting her sister down, the elder girl whispered another incantation:

> "Make of me
> A big thorn tree
> And let my sister
> A small branch be."

The two girls were replaced by a thorn-tree with globules of gum—which had been a string of beads round the elder girl's neck—on its bark. The giants reached the tree and laughed: "One-Eye, you've done it again! The two girls you thought you saw are not what they seemed to be, or has the one sister turned into a tree and the little one into a branch? At least we can eat the gum from the bark." They scraped away the gum and chomped it and because it had the power to put them to sleep seven giants soon lay snoring on the sand. The tree became the two girls again, with gum in their hands which they smeared over the eyelids of the sleeping giants before running across the plain to their village which they knew the giants would never dare attack, for the warriors were fierce and their assegais sharp.

They were safely home when One-Eye awoke, to scrape the gum from his solitary eyelid and roar: "We have been bewitched, my brothers, asleep on the sand, our eyelids gummed together, and the tree gone and with it the two girls. We are humiliated. We shall become the laughing stock of yonder tribe when the two girls tell their story. Listen!"

And, indeed, from far off came the sound of boisterous laughter.

It was this laughter reaching them from across the plain that drove the giants away to live in another part of Africa and never come back to that place, because ridicule has always been the greatest enemy of Evil.

Jungle Hide-and-Seek

This story comes from Southern Nigeria where the legends are very old and have been handed on from generation to generation. It is only during this century that the stories have been written down and translated by, among others, anthropologists and district commissioners.

Early in the morning before the sun brings light to Africa the hush of the night shatters as the bush-fowls screech and the roosters and hens in the kraal crow and cluck in reply. It is part of the eternal pattern of Africa and it began with a game of hide-and-seek. . .

There was a time when all the birds and animals were friends together, with hens and roosters quite unafraid of the eagle and the hawk. Their only enemy was man. Because the eagle could fly very high and then plummet down to warn the animals that man was near, he was elected King of the Air while the small grey antelope was undisputed King of the Land, through his intelligence, keen eyes and superb sense of smell, which enabled him to know more swiftly than the others when man was prowling in the vicinity with his bows and poison-tipped arrows and assegais. Even when he was drinking (which is when an animal is most vulnerable) he could outwit the hunters by watching their coming through the small holes in his feet.

One day, in sport, the eagle challenged the antelope to a hiding contest between bird and animal. "I select the hawk to represent us, and who is your representative?"

The antelope replied that the bush cow would see that the animals were not disgraced by defeat, and it was decided that the hawk would be the first to hide. He did this so successfully—hiding covered by the creepers that had wrapped themselves around a high tree—that the bush cow could not locate him, and the antelope had to accept defeat on behalf of the animals.

86

"Round one to the birds," he said, "but we demand a second chance tomorrow."

Defeated again, the antelope claimed that the one hiding had the advantage, so on the third day the bush cow hid himself, tiptoeing into his favourite mudhole, wallowing until only a small part of his head and back showed above the ooze, looking like two muddy stones. No sooner was he comfortably settled and preparing to spend the day in peaceful sleep than the hawk flew down, danced on his back, plucked out some hair from the top of his head, and flew away laughing because he had known the bush cow's habits so well that locating him had posed no problem at all.

This time the antelope was incensed. "Once more!" he cried, "and the winner of this round will be the champion!"

This time the hawk hid in his creeper-covered tree again, but because the game was beginning to bore him he waited until the bush cow came trotting past beneath him and landed so delicately on his horns that the animal was unaware of his presence throughout the day. Finally, late in the day, tired after seeking everywhere, he came across a number of hens and roosters. "What is so amusing?" he demanded crossly. "Why are you laughing at me? Do you know where the hawk is hiding?" Their uncontrollable laughter stopped abruptly when the bush cow cried out: "If you do not tell me immediately, I shall trample on you!"

In the sudden silence one rooster said, "Shake your head, bush cow," and as he did so he heard the flapping of wings and turning round saw the hawk flying towards a clump of trees.

"We are the victors," boasted the antelope. "I knew we should win in the end." The eagle accepted defeat gracefully, but amiability turned to fierce anger when the hawk told him how he had been betrayed on the horns of the bush cow by the hens and roosters. The eagle immediately flew to where they were pecking nuts and berries in a clearing.

"You have angered me greatly by giving away the hiding-place of the hawk and thereby enabling the animals to defeat the birds in the contest of hide-and-seek. You have betrayed your fellow-birds! You are traitors to the bird cause, and from this day I have given the hawk my royal permission to attack you and your chickens whenever and wherever he finds you." And he stormed off into the skies before they could plead with him to change his cruel decree.

That night they held a conference and made their decision to live with man. "He is our enemy but we shall offer to lay eggs for him and he will become our friend."

Only the bush fowls objected. "Here we were born and here we shall stay, even if we have to live in fear of the hawk's talons. We choose freedom above domesticity." The hens and roosters, too terrified to spend any time converting them, moved off in a great flock to the kraal where man lived and where they believed they would find safety and peace.

Without the clucking hens and the crowing roosters, the bush fowls felt lonely, and shortly afterwards they started what has become an early-morning ritual all over Africa. Early in the morning, before the sun brings light to Africa, the hush of the night shatters as the bush fowls screech, "Hens and roosters, come back to the bush where you belong!"

And the hens cluck and the roosters crow their adamant reply, "No, we have become domesticated and we shall stay with man forever!"

The Ghost of the Mighty Torofini

THE GHOST OF THE MIGHTY TOROFINI is a fine example of the esteem in which the tortoise is held among the Yoruba, Edo and Ibo tribes of Nigeria. Unlike his plodding European counterpart, the tortoise in Nigerian folklore lives by his wits. He is clever and shrewd, and often unscrupulous.

Mihama was renowned for the delicious Akara balls she cooked and sold, not only in her own village but at the market in the town beyond the hills. They were made of meat and corn with chopped herbs and onions to give them flavour, and wherever she went

the wonderful aroma spread out before her to bring
the customers out of their huts before she herself
even reached them.

One day, when she came along the road carrying
on her head a basket of Akara balls to sell at the
market, the tortoise who lived by his wits—which
is a nice way of saying that he lived off others—
was slumbering in his hiding-hole behind a boulder
near the road. He awoke, nostrils twitching, and as
the girl went past he was thinking to himself,
"Tomorrow. Tomorrow. . ."

Long before she reached him on the following
morning he could smell the aroma of the Akara
balls, especially the chopped herbs and the onions
picked fresh from the bushes, and from his hiding-
hole where he could not be seen he heard her singing. . . .

"Akara balls I bring to sell.
O the fragrant onion smell.
Akara balls I make and fry—
To market! To market! Come buy! Come buy!"

When her dancing feet were kicking up little
puffs of dust on the sandy path near him, he began to
sing in the voice that so many had found so irresis-
tible that he had never had to do a day's work in his
life:

"If you're selling beans, I bar the way;
I've stopped four bakers here today.
Torofini I am, the magical King,

91

The world obeys me in everything.
Dance, dance, dance down the road, my dear,
But leave your Akara balls right here
For the ghost of the mighty Torofini."

Putting her basket down like a girl in a dream, she went dancing along the road until the spell snapped and she realised that she had left her merchandise behind her on the path. By the time she got back to where the tortoise had charmed her, the basket was lying where she had left it but empty now, and in his hiding-hole the tortoise was laughing so much that he was almost choking on the wonderful food he had acquired so easily.

Her parents didn't laugh when she told them about the voice that had come out of nowhere. "Singing ghost, indeed!" they snorted. "Tomorrow we shall go with you, to make sure that such foolishness does not empty your basket again. Into the kitchen with you, gullible girl, to make Akara balls for us to sell in the market tomorrow."

The sun was just high enough to make their shadows long on the ground when father, mother and daughter went down the road to market. His nostrils twitching in his hiding-hole, the tortoise began to sing as soon as the three sets of feet were padding on the path very close to where he lay:

"Akara balls came yesterday.
Let them stay again today
For Torofini the magical King,

Obeyed by all who hear him sing.
Leave the Akara balls, I say,
And empty-handed dance away!"

In a trance they did what they were told. The girl's parents were very angry when they came out of their dream and hurried back to where the mysterious voice had bewitched them, to find the baskets empty in the road.

"The King must hear of this!" roared the enraged father, and he made arrangements to see their ruler whose fat body bulged over the sides of his throne where he sat surrounded by the chiefs who stood round their monarch in a wide respectful circle.

As the girl's father told the story, the King became angrier and angrier, and so did the chiefs for part of their function was to reflect the King's moods. "Enough!" he bellowed, his fat quivering body causing his throne to creak. "Enough!" echoed the chiefs before the King lifted his hand for silence and said: "Your King has a plan as noble as the royal blood that placed him on his throne to rule wisely over his subjects. Mihama, make more Akara balls, sweeter than ever with chopped onions and herbs, and tomorrow your King, your chiefs and all of you will march to the market to the incessant beating of the tribal drums. In this way the voice of Torofini will be drowned by our noise and the market will thrill again to the cry of "Akara balls for sale!"

Next morning the procession marched out of the village—the quivering bellowing King, his sturdy chiefs, Mihama and her parents, and ahead of them six drummers setting up a ceaseless tattoo, their hands and fingers dancing on the tight ox-hides.

The tortoise heard the drumming swelling out of the distance, and then he could smell the aroma of the Akara balls and see the marching feet raising the sand of the road into dust. He began to sing, with throbbing voice, louder than the drumming:

> "Dance to the drum
> Away to the hill
> But I must stay
> And eat my fill.
> King and chiefs, one and all,
> Put down every Akara ball.
> You, my friends, will not eat any:
> They are all for the mighty Torofini."

Everybody was in a rage when they came out of their dream and returned to the empty basket on the road. The tortoise was rolling about in his hiding-hole, laughing so uncontrollably that he couldn't start eating until the King's party had dwindled to mere specks in the distance.

Mihama did not go to the market next day. The King was dejected because he had been outwitted by a power greater than his own, and the chiefs were suitably glum, listlessly surrounding their ruler. On the third day a wise man was ushered into the King's presence. What he said to the King was enough to make him rumble and quiver with laughter. The chiefs, of course, found it equally amusing. "Command Mihama to make Akara balls in abundance!" he cried; and to the wise man he said, "Tell your brother Motilo to be ready to march with us in the morning."

With the sun behind them, their shadows led them down the road to where the tortoise waited. Smelling the aroma of the Akara balls, his hiding-hole vibrating with the drumming and the thudding feet, he began to sing, even more loudly than before:

> "Torofini banishes words today
> Because he is hungry. Scamper away
> To where midday will find you
> But leave the Akara balls
> Behind you."

He smiled in triumph to see them putting down the sweet-smelling baskets before dancing and drumming down the road towards the hill, and he came out of his hiding-hole to stand laughing at the baskets of Akara balls. He stopped laughing when a shadow fell across him and he was grabbed and held from behind. Desperately he sang again:

> "Dance from here, flee from me!
> Obey the commands of Torofini,
> As all your other friends have done.
> Leave my presence and run, man, run!"

But the grip only tightened. And then the tortoise

found himself surrounded by King and chiefs, Mihama, her parents, and the drummers, and the King was saying, pompously: "So this is the mighty Torofini! Well, I have captured you so I am mightier than you. I suppose you'd like to know how we did it, eh, tortoise? Well, when your singing charmed us, Motilo here stayed behind and captured you when you came out to eat your ill-gotten Akara balls. I suppose you're wondering why he didn't hear your song. Motilo, my dear tortoise, is deaf! And he and his brother will return to their village tomorrow laden with gifts."

Of course they put the tortoise on trial for his life. "Let it be at night," he pleaded, "for the sunshine hurts my eyes so much that I will not be able to see the King." The stars were spangles in the sky and the moon was in full sail when they pronounced sentence on the tortoise. "You shall die for your sins," roared the King; and at that moment the tortoise's voice filled the night:

"Torofini commands you, stay where you are.
Focus your eyes on a distant star.
Next time you catch him, try him by day
For night will take him far away."

And by the time the charm wore off, he had vanished in the darkness, and all their searching was in vain. In that part of Africa it is not surprising that it is not only the animals who regard the tortoise as being an exceedingly clever fellow!

96

The Hawk and the Chickens

This story is unique to Southern Nigeria where 1,500,000 Ibibio people share a common language and a culture which is typically West African.

Long ago, the story goes in Africa, a young and beautiful hen lived in the bush with her parents, pecking corn, listening to the rooster's cry rousing the morning and urging the sun to awake and pour its light across the horizon.

One morning, with the sun fully awake, and the rooster, his daily work done, asleep in the shade of a baobab tree, a shadow swept back and forth across the ground as a hawk circled above, coming nearer with every large and easy circle, until he settled flapping on a nearby fence. Coyly, the hen gazed at the big bird.

"Good morning, adorable hen," he said. "You do not know me but I have watched you often from the heights of the heavens and now I love you and wish to marry you and carry you away to my nest my eyrie in the Mountains of Mitsikamakizi. Well, what is your answer, angelic hen?"

Her answer was swift and definite, and in no time at all the hawk had discussed the matter with her parents, paid the dowry—enough corn to keep the family pecking for many months—and led her away to his high home in the Mountains of Mitsikamakizi where they lived happily together.

Some months afterwards, when the dowry of corn had dwindled to a mere basketful, a young rooster came to visit the hen's parents. "I have been long away," he said, "and now I have come back home, to marry your daughter, but I cannot see her. Where can I find her?"

He was disappointed to learn that she had become the wife of a hawk but because he was very determined and much in love he decided that he would seek her out and bring her back. Dawn was red in the sky when he set out, his crowing like a bugle-blast, his comb and plumage a golden shimmer in the sunlight. At last he found the hawk's nest lofty in the mountains and began to woo the hen who was sitting in the nest while her husband was circling the plains seeking food. She remembered her childhood playmate very well, and she had known much loneliness up there in the mountains away from her own kind; and the food the hawk provided was not often to her liking, so she agreed to renounce her husband and marry the rooster.

Next morning the hawk flew angrily to the court of the King of all the Birds, the bald-headed hump-shouldered vulture, dressed in black and looking as if the problems of the world were his personal responsibility. When the hawk had told his story, hopping up and down and flapping his huge wings gustily in his anger, the King called for the parents of the hen, chided them for her behaviour and ordered them to pay back the dowry of corn given to them by the hawk for his bride.

"We are too poor, your Majesty," said her father, "and we have, in any case, eaten all the corn. What there is left would not even provide shelter for the smallest insect."

"In that case," screeched the vulture, his red bald head flushing even redder, "I give the hawk and all hawks who come after him permission to kill and eat your children and their children and their children's children from this day until time itself stops. That right will make up for the lost dowry."

The father argued that the punishment was too savage for the offence, and that it was cruelly unjust to visit the sins of one generation upon those who had not yet been born, but the vulture's verdict was unalterable. Sadly and silently, the rooster and his wife flew back home, knowing that their lives had changed for the worse.

As a result, many hens and roosters sought refuge from the curse by going to live with man as domesticated animals, while the more courageous among them stayed in the bush as wild fowl. And ever since that day of judgement, whenever a hawk circling high in the sky sees a chicken on the ground, in the bush or on a farm, his shadow grows larger as he swoops down to claim his right, his dowry.

Sun and Moon and Water

Another story from Nigeria; part of the folklore of the Efik-Ibibio, a subsidiary Ibibio tribe many of whose members are fishermen.

A million years ago and more, when the only life was in the sea and the first man had yet to walk upon the earth and the birds to fly darting above it, the Sun and the Moon lived together in Africa as husband and wife.

One day the Sun said to his good friend the Water,

"Why is it that although I am constantly visiting you, not once have you been a guest in my house?"

"Ah," gurgled the Water in reply, "I should love to come to your house because you are my dearest friend and I long to meet your wife the Moon. But your house is too small to accommodate me and those who come with me as part of me wherever I flow—shellfish, starfish, the pretty little butterfly fish, the shoals of sardines and swarms of mackerel, the sharp-toothed shark and the whale who is the mightiest of all. If you had a huge kraal, I should visit you with pleasure, again and again."

"In the name of friendship I shall build a kraal big enough for you and all of yours, and invite you as soon as it is ready," said the Sun; and when, later, his beaming wife the Moon opened the door to him, he told her what had happened and immediately started building a kraal so vast that it extended beyond the horizon in all directions. Then, when all was complete, he invited the Water to be his guest at last.

They saw the Water moving along from many miles away, flowing across the plains, among the trees, around the hills, until he was swirling about their ankles, saying, "Here I am, dear Sun, happy to be here, glad to be meeting your wife the Moon at last. And what a big and beautiful place you have built so that I could visit you."

By the time he had said all this, the Sun and the Moon were knee-deep in the Water sparkling with fishes big and small. "We're not all here yet," bubbled the Water. "Can you accommodate the rest of us?"

"It goes without saying," smiled the Sun. "Without a doubt," the Moon beamed. And the water kept coming, and rising. Now the sharks and the turtles were there, the flying fishes were flashing in the air, and the whales broke the surface of the Water and fell back with a crash. By now the Sun and Moon were perched atop their highest roof; and when the Water gargled again, "Can you accommodate the rest of us?" the Moon whispered fearfully, "I believe you're filling our kraal to overflowing," but the Sun said that was nonsense and cried out, "You're welcome! Our kraal is large enough for everybody."

But it wasn't; and very soon the Water was flowing over the top of the roof and would have engulfed the Sun and the Moon if they had not jumped into the sky with such fright and desperation that their leap carried them millions of miles away to where they could look back on the earth as being no bigger than a smallish plum. "I told you he was filling our kraal to overflowing," were the last plaintive words the Moon spoke on the earth.

Up in the sky they built a home where they reared the many children—called stars—that were born to them after they had left the earth. Although their children the stars numbered many thousands, the parents knew each one of them by name, and they were a pretty happy family except on those occasions when the Moon yearned to be back on the earth again and murmured plaintively, "I told you he was filling our kraal to overflowing."

When she said this for the ten-thousandth time, the Sun became so angry that he tried to beat his wife. Their argument shattered the heavens and started the first volcanoes rumbling down on the earth. Afterwards, when all was quiet and the Sun was sleeping, the Moon gathered all her children together and took them far away, to another part of the limitless sky.

After sulking alone for some days, the Sun began to feel lonely and set out to seek his wife the Moon and the stars his children. Every day he used up all his energy to burn his brightest and light up the sky so that he could see them; and in the evening, weary and weak from his endeavours, he would sink down in the west. It was then that the Moon would bring her children out from hiding, to dance across the sky, twinkling and glittering in the heavens while she beamed benignly over their caperings.

And every morning just before the Sun—refreshed by sleep and burning brightly again—came bounding up in the east of the African sky, the Moon would call her stars together and they would run away and hide on the other side of the world until the Sun was once again setting red-faced and exhausted in the west.

"When he sets in the west," the storytellers say

at campfires in many parts of Africa, the flames dancing in their eyes, the sparks crackling upwards to join the stars, "she comes out with her children. And when her husband comes looking for her, she runs away, today, tomorrow, forever."

No Bats in the Daytime

The tortoise is once again the hero in this tale told by the Ibibio people.

"Mother lamb," said the bat, "I am going to visit my father-in-law and I wonder whether one of your seven lambs would like to come with me, to carry my drinking horn and see something of the world—the rolling hills and high mountains, forests and rivers, and so on. It will be quite an experience for whichever one of them decides to accompany me."

"Let me go, mother," the youngest lamb bleated, "for I am yearning to travel the open road and see the world."

And carrying the drinking horn, he waved goodbye to his family and trotted off down the road with the bat in the early morning. Halfway to his father-in-law's, the bat told the lamb to leave the horn under a bamboo tree, and as soon as they reached their destination he sent the lamb back to collect it. The lamb was tired and hungry when he finally arrived in the gloaming and very disappointed when the bat said, "You've taken so long to return that we've eaten everything. Have a drink from the horn."

For the next four days the innocent lamb was a victim of the bat's guile. He was sent to place the drinking horn under the bamboo tree and when he came back only the crumbs remained from the evening meal. And when he was sent to retrieve the horn, the same pattern repeated itself. By the time the bat took him back to his mother's he was thin with hunger and when she heard his story she stamped and bleated in her rage and rushed off to tell the wily tortoise what had happened.

"Leave it to me, madam," he murmured.

It wasn't long before the bat called again, off to his father-in-law and burbling of the open road and seeing the world and how educational the trip would be for "one of the dear innocent lambs".

"We're expecting relatives from over the hills,"

said the mother lamb, "so my children must stay at home," and the tortoise came plodding out from behind a bush and offered to help the bat, who gave him the drinking horn to carry and they moved off down the road. Halfway there, with the sun directly overhead announcing the middle of the day, the bat told the tortoise to leave the horn under a bamboo tree, but the wily plodder only pretended to do so and put it in the sack he was carrying. As soon as they reached bat's father-in-law the tortoise hid the horn behind a bush.

The stew in the calabash suspended over the fire smelled so good that the tortoise's beak was chattering in anticipation.

"Be a good fellow and fetch my drinking horn," said the bat, and the tortoise obediently plodded away towards the sunset. "He won't be back for ages," he heard the bat say as he reached the bush. "Now we can eat and when he comes back we shall have finished everything." But their laughter turned to silent disbelief and consternation as they heard a voice saying, "Here is your drinking horn, bat, and with it a hungry tortoise." The bat was so angry that he stalked away without eating, and his appetite left him for four days, making him thin while the tortoise became fat.

On the fifth day his appetite returned with intolerable pangs of hunger. "Bring my food to the hut," he said to his father-in-law. "When it is ready, wake me; I want to sleep for a while." Hearing this, the tortoise entered the hut, carried the sleeping bat to the other bed, and slipping into the bat's bed he covered himself with the blankets.

Soon the bat's father-in-law put the food down, gently shook what he assumed was his son-in-law and left the hut. The tortoise ate the food, leaving just a little which he placed on the bat's lips after he had carried him back to his own bed. Chuckling appreciatively, he went to sleep himself, after cleaning his teeth thoroughly.

He was awakened by the shrill and angry cries of the bat who was arguing with his father-in-law. "Where is my food?"

"I gave it to you last night and you ate it. See, the bowl is empty."

"Nonsense, I am still starving. Food has not passed my lips. The tortoise must have eaten it. Tortoise, why did you eat my food?"

By this time the shouting had brought some of the neighbours into the doorway, and the tortoise pretended to be much angered by the accusation. "We shall rinse our mouths with water and see which one of us has eaten the food," he announced.

Tortoise and bat did this as the people cried, "Bat ate the food. He is guilty. Tortoise is innocent." And they mocked the bat who fled from them in his shame and anger and was never again seen during the day because after his humiliation he came out only in the darkness of the night.

The tortoise returned to the lamb's family and

said, "Madam, the bat has been punished for the mean tricks he played on one of your lambs and he'll never come by here again with his stories of the open road and the experience of seeing the world with him."

And as the years, and indeed the centuries, went by, the fame of the tortoise and his shrewdness spread far and wide while the bat became more and more a figure of mockery and contempt. So it is to this day in many parts of Africa.

Tall One's Warrior

The incredibly tall, high-jumping warriors of the Masai tribe know this story well. They inhabit Kenya and Northern Uganda. Their cattle play an important role in Masai culture, and each cow is given its own name. Milk is venerated, and every Masai will regulate his diet so that milk and meat do not mix in his stomach.

Tired after the long day's hunt for food, the hare shambled into his hut, the interior dark with the oncoming night. Glistening in the gloom was a trail on the ground.

"Who has come uninvited into my house?" shouted the hare, trembling.

The voice that boomed out of the darkness rattled the reeds of the hut and the calabashes that stood in one corner:

> "Tall One's warrior son I am,
> My anklets graze the ground
> After the fight at the Kwengo Dam
> Where I smashed the rhino to the sand
> And the elephant's girth
> Crashed to the earth
> With a mighty sound,
> And the lions were falling all around!"

The hare scampered outside to find an ally bigger than himself. "Jackal, help me, friend!" he cried. "There is a destroyer in the darkness of my hut and I am afraid."

"You've come to the right animal," boasted the jackal, "for I fear nobody, not even the elephant. Lead me to the upstart who has dared to invade your home and I shall deal with him as I deal with my own enemies."

Swaggering into the hut, his tail swishing, his sharp teeth clashing, he shouted out: "Who is the rogue who offends the nostrils of jackal's friend the hare? Speak!"

The voice boomed in the darkness:

> "A lion I've eaten for supper,
> An elephant I've gobbled for tea,

112

But a jackal in the evening
Will be a new taste for me.
Advance and be beaten!
Come to be eaten!"

After the jackal had fled screaming across the sand, the hare urged the leopard to lend his strength and authority to banishing the intruder. "I who should have been King of the Beasts will be your saviour, little hare," he murmured before entering the hut in a charge. Trembling outside, the hare heard the leopard roaring his challenge, and when the echo had died, rumbling away, the stranger's voice boomed again:

"At Kwengo Dam the dust rose high
Up into the African sky
And when I saw my way again
There were twenty leopards on the plain—
Groaning,
Moaning.
Lying there,
Dying there."

A long line of dust signalled the flashing paws of the retreating leopard; and now the hare sought help from one of the biggest animals of all, the rhinoceros whose armour-plated bulk thundered across the sand to stop just inside hare's hut with the dust swirling around his mightiness. From outside the hare heard him challenging the stranger: "Who dares to molest the tiny hare will be trampled by the hooves of the tremendous awe-inspiring rhinoceros. Come, flee, strange one, or stay to fight and die!"

Hare's heart was trembling with mingled fear and excitement as he waited for the reply:

"Where are the rhinoes of Kwengo Dam?
Where are they today?
Where are they
Who once held sway?
Defeated,
Depleted.
Fled,
Dead!"

The rhino swept through the door, and dust clouds rumbled across the plains with his swift retreat. So the hare approached the biggest animal of all. "Massive elephant, help me to banish the intruder from my hut, you who are so immense and majestic that all the animals fear and respect you."

"I've heard of the fellow's boasting," said the elephant, waving his trunk disdainfully above the hare on the sand far below him, "and of course I don't believe a word of it, and I would love to help you, only I have a bad cold and a running trunk and a touch of rheumatism in my back legs. And there's not much room for manoeuvring in that hut of yours, is there, not for a big fellow like me, anyway? Another time, perhaps, dear hare."

Disgusted, the hare was about to retort when a frog came flying through the air and plopped on the sand beside him. "I heard it all," he said. "Take me to your hut. I'll evict the stranger through the powerful reverberations of my croaking voice. Come!"

Hop! Hop! Plop! The frog was inside the hut, and without waiting for the stranger's booming challenge he uttered his own, swelling himself up to create deep and hollow tones: "I am strong and ugly and unafraid. My food I hunt and kill with a flick of my tongue. I am feared by all my enemies, and I am bigger and stronger than you, stranger, whoever you are. So leave hare's hut before harm can come to you!"

After the echo of his voice had throbbed away, a small voice said in the silence: "If you promise not to touch me, I shall go away, never to cause mischief in these parts again."

The hare jumped out of the shadow and shouted out to the other animals—standing fearfully some distance away in the near darkness—what the unknown stranger had suggested. They agreed.

"Come out, Tall One's warrior son, let us see you, and go in peace," he said through the door.

A caterpillar came humping through the door, and without another boastful word moved away in the growing darkness of the night. . . .

King of the Earth and the Water

Ashantiland is now the southern half of the independent state of Ghana, on the Gold Coast. Between the seventeenth and nineteenth centuries, the Ashantis, with their military prowess and distinctive civilisation, conquered all the neighbouring tribes. They consistently defeated the British in minor battles throughout the nineteenth century and were finally beaten themselves in 1874. Ashantiland became a British colony in 1901.

Expecting her first child, the wife of Chief Ndala-simbi lost her appetite for all food—except fish fresh from the river, so Katumna her servant was commissioned to go fishing every day. When he flung his net into the water, it was jerked under, and no matter how hard he tugged he could not pull it out again.

"Let go, let go, whatever you are!" he cried, "for I have been sent by Chief Ndalasimbi whose wife is heavy with child and whose only diet is fish fresh from the river." And at that moment his net was freed suddenly and he fell over backwards as he pulled it out of the water. To his astonishment, and fear, a strange figure stepped out of the net, a fish with arms and legs and the head of a man, and reaching only as high as his knees. "Who are you?" quavered Katumna.

The voice that answered had music in it, like water sliding over pebbles, tinkling into a pool from a low waterfall, rippling into circles when a small stone is dropped into it. "I am the Lord of the Land, King of the Earth and Water, and no fish will you catch with your net until Chief Ndalasimbi and his wife come to see me here on the riverbank. Go, and fetch them to me!" The strange creature disappeared. Katumna rushed away with his message.

Dressed in their finest robes and accompanied by the wise old men of the kraal, Chief Ndalasimbi and his wife came to the river. "Lord of the Land," the Chief addressed the water, "I have come at your bidding." The strange little figure, part-fish and part-man, rose from the river and stood before them on the bank, saying in his voice of music,

"When you built your kraal in the valley you built in my domains for I am Lord of the Land, King of the Earth and Water. Now your wife wants fish fresh from the river and can eat nothing else. Your servant Katumna I give permission to catch fish for her every day. But if the child is a girl she must become my wife, and if a son he will be my son also and must be named Lukala, after me." And then he became part of the river again.

When their son was born, they named him Lukala and then promptly forgot about the Lord of the Land and what he had said. The boy grew up to be strong and brave and intelligent, but he knew fear one night when he heard a voice of music speaking in his dreams: "Lukala must come to live in the river with Lukala his other father, Lord of the Land, King of the Earth and the Water. If he does not obey me, he will surely die!"

"I have been expecting something like this for some time," his father said when Lukala had related his dream. "You must leave this place, my son, and go as far away as you can. I shall give you two each of bulls to ride on, goats and pigs and chickens for sustenance, and dogs to be your guides and companions. But you must never cross a river, for the Lord of the Land will be lying in wait for you there. Rather must you follow a river to its very source, a spring in the mountains, so that you go around it instead of across it. Go well, my son. May we all meet again before too many years of absence."

118

On the fifth day of his journey he emerged from the bush into a clearing that was teeming with land and river animals, birds, even insects. Every one of God's creatures seemed to be represented there. Fearlessly, Lukala pushed his way through to the centre where the lion was standing over the body of an antelope. "Ah, Lukala," he roared as if he had been expecting the young man to arrive at that very moment, "help us in our problem. We have to divide this animal into enough pieces to give every animal, bird and insect here a share. Our teeth and claws are clumsy instruments in comparison with your sharp-bladed knife." But when Lukala had meticulously divided the meat into sufficient tiny portions to go round, hunger still reigned in the clearing, and as the animals were now looking hungrily at him, he slaughtered his own bulls, goats, pigs and chickens (the two dogs he had given to a chief who had given him hospitality along the way), divided the meat into many portions and shared them out among animals, birds, and insects.

"Your generosity will be rewarded," said the lion. "Stand upon this tree-stump and one by one we shall pledge our future help. For myself, I say to you that if you find yourself in trouble, the call of 'Telezi, King of the Beasts, I invoke your aid' will reach my ears." And the animals lined up to address Lukala, thus:

"On your day of need, say 'Telezi, wolf of the assegai'."

"Should misfortune envelop you, call 'Telezi, leopard'."

"The cry of 'Telezi, jackal' will remove distress from your shoulders."

"When hardship slows down your progress in the world, shout 'Telezi, hawk, the bird who can catch a child'."

"When you want the stars to be your neighbours, call 'Telezi, eagle, the bird who lost his tailfeathers flying too close to the sun'."

They all came up to Lukala, even the tiny ant who said, " 'Telezi, little ant, I need your mighty power'." And as the young man prepared to continue his wanderings, the clearing became bare, emptied of all life.

He could now ignore his father's warning about crossing rivers, because he could become a hawk at will, and when he was hungry he turned himself into a leopard and stole into a kraal to kill a couple of fowls, but the guards heard the commotion and he fled into the darkness, turning himself into a man again, with two roosters hanging from the staff he carried over his shoulder.

"No, I haven't seen a leopard," he replied when the villagers met him on the road. "I was taking these two roosters to my brother in the kraal over the hill when they died on the road, so I shall cook and eat them." As he approached the next village hunger came on him again so he became a wolf and stole two succulent pigs, once again escaping into the darkness. But the next transformation brought disaster.

As a wolf, he stole two pigs, became a man again, cooked and ate the meat and fell asleep. Two maidens from the village fetching water on the following morning saw him sleeping surrounded by the remains of the pigs, and returned to their village saying, "Was it a wolf who killed the two pigs or the young man we saw sleeping beside the road, the fire cold grey ashes and around him the bones of the two pigs?"

Armed with sticks and staves and cowhide shields, the young men of the village marched along the road, stamping and chanting, waking the young man who waited until their leader was an elephant's length from him before he cried out, "Telezi, King of the Beasts, I invoke your aid!" One earth-shaking roar was all it needed to send the warriors scurrying and scampering back to their kraal, and as he turned himself into Lukala again he was still shaking with laughter.

Soon he came to the greatest kraal in Angola, ruled over by the mighty Mosi Tunya himself. A hawk, he circled high above the kraal. Then, a tiny bird with gorgeous plumage, he was darting and swooping above the Chief's residence. At that moment Chini, the Chief's beautiful daughter, came out into the sunshine, her eyes dazzled by the plumage of the little bird. "How can I catch the beautiful bird?" she asked her handmaidens. "I have

121

never seen anything so lovely in all my days." Neither had Lukala; so when she sat on the grass he fluttered down beside her. Very gently, she held out her hand, calling him sweetly, and he hopped on to her palm. "Father!" she cried, carrying the bird into the Chief's house, "Here is a bird beautiful enough to live in my golden cage that has never known an occupant." Lukala found himself inside a cage of gold swinging from the roof. They gave him rice and water which he tasted but couldn't eat because although he had become a bird he was still Lukala and his stomach called for more substantial fare than rice and water. To make matters worse, there was a long table below him covered with marvellous food—meat and fish, mangoes and pawpaws—but the handmaidens were always on duty there.

When they left the room late that night to sleep, Lukala was ravenously hungry. "Telezi, little ant, I need your mighty power," he chirruped as softly as he could, and if the maidens had been there they would have seen an ant climbing slowly up the rope and down the wall, then turning miraculously into a man, voraciously eating everything on the table, becoming an ant again, climbing laboriously back into the cage and becoming a marvellously plum-aged bird again.

But of course nobody saw these transformations, so nobody knew who the mysterious intruder was who cleared the table of the Chief's food in the middle of the night. The maidens were blamed and protested their innocence with angry tears. And Chini was sad because after three days the water in the cage had not been drunk and the rice was hardly ruffled. "The bird will die," she said. "If he has not eaten by the morning I shall set him free. He came into my palm and into the cage so willingly, but perhaps he yearns for the freedom of the skies— and the danger, for hawks and eagles must surely be his enemies."

Lukala was touched by her compassion, but the maids were angered by the unjust accusation that they could possibly be the thieves, so that night they hid themselves in the next room and watched through the open door.

"Mistress," they said next morning, "you won't believe what we are going to tell you, but it is true. That bird has magic powers, becoming an insect to escape from the cage, a man to eat all the food—and such a fine looking young man!—and once again an insect to climb back into the cage and become a bird again. So we are not thieves and the bird will not die of hunger even if it leaves the rice and water untouched."

Of course Chini did not believe this outrageous excuse, so on the next night she joined her hand-maidens and was astonished to find that their story was true. As the young man swallowed the last mouthful of paw-paw, Chini appeared in the door-way. They needed no more than the light of the full moon to know that they were in love, and in the morning Lukala told his story to the Chief and said he wished to marry Chini and take her with him to his father's kraal. "If she wishes it, you may marry her, Lukala, son of Ndalasimbi, but before we even discuss these matters I must beg a service of you."

"Anything, mighty Mosi Tunya, anything," said the eager young man.

"There is a sadness in our lives," said Mosi Tunya. "A long time ago our enemies defeated us and took my younger daughter away with them. Even though she is a Chief's daughter, they have made a servant of her, and she is the one who throws the dead ashes of the fires on to a big heap outside the kraal every morning. They are very far from here, across three mountain ranges, a river and a lake, which is why we have been unable to recapture her and bring her back to her own people."

His last words were still lingering in the air when Lukala was crying out urgently, "Telezi, eagle, the bird who lost his tail feathers flying too close to the sun!" And the huge wings flapped up the dust and lifted the bird into the sky. Mosi Tunya and Chini, shielding their eyes from the sun, watched until the eagle was a speck, and even when they could no longer see even that they continued gazing into the sky, the father wishing for his daughter, Chini wishing for her sister and longing for the young man to return. Slowly, without saying a word, they walked back to their house.

Spread out below Lukala were mountains and hills, forests, the meadows with rivers cutting through them glinting in the sunshine. Whenever a wisp of smoke told him that he was flying above a kraal, he swooped down to see if he could find the girl who threw the ashes on a heap. When he was tired he became a hawk, and then an eagle again, and at night he came down to the earth, close to a kraal, stole pigs or chickens as a wolf or a lion or a leopard, and became a man to cook and eat the meat. He was yearning to get back to the beautiful Chini, and every night at his campfire he knew loneliness as he had never experienced it before.

Many days and many villages later, he came down out of the skies to investigate a wisp of smoke, and he saw a young girl almost as lovely as Chini emptying the ashes on to a heap just outside the kraal. "How shall I rescue her?" he was thinking in his circling. "To become a hawk and swoop down and carry her off would be to terrify her out of her wits." And even as he watched her going back into the hut, an assegai whistling past him made him fly with great speed to rest on the very pinnacle of a nearby mountain.

During the night he planned his campaign. Early in the morning an eagle dropped out of the sky and came to rest outside the kraal, turning immediately into a goat which trotted towards the girl's hut while the whole village was still asleep. Hearing a flurry of wings, he looked up in terror to see a hawk bearing down on him, and as the bird's cruel talons were about to plunge into him he managed to turn himself into an ant, and the mystified hawk flew hungrily away.

But now the ground was trembling violently about him, and so was he, as a huge form loomed over him, its sharp beak pecking at the ground and coming ever closer. A hen! In a flash he had turned himself into a rooster, and the hen ran crazily in all directions, clucking and squawking hideously, and all around the people began to stir. The sun would soon be up. Already the horizon glowed red.

Inside the girl's hut he crowed mightily, and she awoke to see a young man standing in the doorway. "Do not scream," he said. "I have come from your father to bring you home. Get up immediately and run as fast as you can. A hawk will carry you away, but do not be afraid. And ask me no questions. Hurry! Now!"

Mutely, the girl did as she was told, running out of her hut, through the gateway, and into the bush. Before Lukala could move, the red horizon was blotted out by a warrior brandishing a spear and crying, "Interloper! Rescuer of our captive! Die!" As he hurled his assegai, the hut exploded into a thousand pieces and trumpeting shrilly with ears flapping an elephant lumbered across the open space between the huts with bits of wood and straw falling from him.

By now four warriors pursuing the girl were

almost upon her, and from every doorway men were swarming. The elephant's trumpeting scattered them, and as the terrified girl fell to the ground with the elephant's shadow over her she saw the earth spinning away below her and her body was heavy in her clothes that were being held by the talons of a hawk. Then her clothes began to tear with a terrible ripping sound, and just in time, before she could fall through the sky to her death, the hawk hovered above a tree and she clung to a branch and climbed down to the ground, to be met by the young man who had rescued her.

Becoming a hawk, then a jackal, he stole a blanket, and when the hawk returned to her the girl wrapped herself in the blanket and the big bird carried her back to her father's kraal, where she served as the radiant maid-of-honour at her sister Chini's wedding to Lukala.

Cat on a Velvet Cushion

Like KING OF THE EARTH AND THE WATER, this story forms part of the heritage of the Ashanti people.

Because of what happened there many hundreds of years ago, cats are pampered and petted in certain parts of Ashantiland while dogs receive the remnants of affection and the left-overs of food. It all began when the youthful Aku asked his mother for

128

some gold-dust to enable him to visit the distant coast and buy salt.

But when he came home again he had no salt, only a dog which he had bought from a man he had met along the way. His mother gave him some more gold-dust and he set out again, only to meet a man with a cat for sale, "this wonderful animal that always lands on its feet".

A third time he set out with a small bag of gold-dust, and on this occasion the man he encountered carried a pigeon in a cage. There was something about the bird, its noble poise and air of authority, that made the youth buy it when the man said it was for sale. Of course his mother scolded him for throwing away all their gold, but she loved her son so much that she never mentioned his foolishness again. So mother and son, cat, dog and pigeon lived harmoniously together.

One morning, shortly after Aku had changed the water and put grain in the pigeon's foodbowl, the bird spoke to him: "Aku, my lad, it was kind of you to buy me and rescue me from the man who had stolen me away from my people. In return, let me show my gratitude. Although I am a pigeon I am the chief of a tribe. Take me back to my people and they will thank you with blessings and gifts."

Aku was impressed by the fact that the bird could speak, but he had grown in wisdom so he replied: "That you are a chief I find hard to believe. No doubt, as soon as I open the door of your cage you will fly away and I shall not see you again, nor hear your cooing at the rising and setting of the sun."

"Well said!" replied the pigeon. "You are learning from experience. But to show you how honest I am I suggest you tie a string to my leg so that I will be unable to fly away, perched on your shoulder while we go together to my people."

They came to a big kraal where the children who were playing marbles in the dust stopped their game and ran towards the biggest hut crying, "Queen Mother, our chief has returned!" A moment later many warriors surrounded Aku and carried him shoulder-high into the large hut where the Queen Mother greeted the pigeon and thanked Aku for bringing him home again. After the celebrating and the feasting, all the people formed a circle round the Queen Mother on her throne, the pigeon on his tiny throne, and Aku standing before them.

"Take this pot of gold," the pigeon said, "for your kindness; and this ring from the Queen Mother's finger which will give you anything you may desire. Farewell, Aku."

When he came home he told his mother what had happened, and placing the ring on the ground he said, "Ring, clear the bush and forest away!" And the forest and bush retreated, leaving a great flat open space.

"Ring, take this old hut away and in its place put many houses!" And they were surrounded by dwellings.

"Ring, bring people to live in these houses, and let them have sheep and cattle, and implements to till the soil!" And the huts buzzed with conversation and a vast herd of cattle stood outside the gate waiting to come in. "Hail, chief!" the people greeted Aku, and to his mother, "Hail, Queen Mother!" And they prospered mightily.

Now, Aku had a friend called Kwaku Ananse who was a spider, and one day when Kwaku Ananse visited him he told him of the magic ring that had brought him his fortune. Back at his own kraal, the crafty Ananse said to his niece, a truly beautiful girl, "Visit Aku and his mother and steal the magic ring he has on his finger." She visited them and was overwhelmed by their generous hospitality, but this did not prevent her from stealing the ring when Aku left it on a table before going down to the river to bathe.

While he was looking everywhere for his lost property, the news came to him that Kwaku Ananse had of a sudden built a town even bigger than his own, but even then he did not suspect the spider and his beautiful niece for the loss of his ring.

Soon afterwards, when Aku was walking along the road, an old bearded man sitting in the shade of a tree said to him: "Seek not to know who I am, for I am not mortal, but listen to what I have to say: It was Kwaku Ananse's beautiful niece who stole your ring. Let it be known that you intend sending your cat and dog to retrieve your property so that Kwaku Ananse will place meat containing a drug in their path which they, being aware of, will not eat and so get your ring back for you." Before Aku could reply he was standing alone. The old man had vanished.

After Aku had cunningly spread the rumour that he knew Kwaku Ananse had the ring and that he would be sending his cat and dog to return it to its rightful owner, he spoke to the two animals: "Ever since I bought you, along the road to the sea, I have treated you well. Here is your chance to do something for me. A ring has been stolen from me by the niece of Kwaku Ananse the spider. It is in a box on the table in his hut in the new town which the magic ring created for him, as it created this town for me. Will you help me?"

Cat and dog nodded their heads in agreement and Aku continued: "I want you to fetch that ring and bring it back. But when you come across some meat in your path on the way to his house, do not touch it for it contains a drug to make you sleep and has been placed there to tempt you."

Cat and dog moved swiftly in the direction of Kwaku Ananse's town, swimming across the river and then walking briskly along the path until they came to the temptingly flavoured meat. The cat immediately sprang over it but the dog, sniffing it, claimed he had a cramp in his stomach and would have to rest a while. As soon as he saw the cat disappearing around the bend in the road, he gobbled up the meat. . .

The cat entered Kwaku Ananse's house unseen and jumped on to a beam above the table. He could see the box on the table, but it was locked. Next to it stood a loaf of bread, and a ball of string. Soon a mouse crawled along the tabletop and as it started nibbling the bread the cat dropped down from the beam and seized the mouse who squeaked in dismay, "Cat, spare my life and I will do your bidding!"

"Nibble through this box and give me the ring that lies inside it, and I shall let you go."

"I agree. Take your paws off me and let me set to work."

"But you will scamper away as soon as I release you."

"Tie this string around my body so that I will be unable to escape."

And with the string round his body, the mouse gnawed and nibbled at the box until he had made a hole big enough for him to slip through. Disappearing through it, he emerged with the ring in his teeth. The cat took it, slipped the string from the mouse's body, purred his thanks and sped back to where he had left the dog. He found him sleeping and the meat gone. When he tapped the dog on the shoulder he awoke to open his eyes and yawn mightily.

"You are lying where I left you, but what has become of the meat that was here when we came?"

"I do not know, for I fell asleep to ease the agony in my stomach. Perhaps somebody took it away, or some other animal may have eaten it. But tell me, cat, where is the ring for our master?"

"I have it here. While you were sleeping, I collected it."

"Give it to me, good friend. You will have difficulty swimming across the river and may drop it in the water, whereas I am a good swimmer so it will be safe with me."

The cat agreed, and while they were swimming across the river the dog, still feeling the effects of the drugged meat, opened his mouth to yawn and the ring fell into the water. The cat immediately sank to the bottom, following the falling ring which was snatched up by a passing fish which was astonished to find itself held fast by a cat who had no right to be wandering about on the riverbed. "Give me that ring you've swallowed," bubbled the cat, "or I shall kill you." In its fear the fish coughed and spluttered and the cat grabbed the ring as it emerged from the fish's mouth and he swam up to the surface and scrambled on to the bank. The dog was nowhere to be seen. . . .

Aku was surprised and delighted to see his pet again for the dog had told him that the cat had been drowned, taking the ring with him. He put the ring on his finger and turned to address the dog who was beginning to slink out of the hut. "Dog," he said, "you have disobeyed me and failed me. From now on you and your descendants in these parts will live on the leavings and find your own place for sleeping."

And to the cat he said: "Whatever I eat I shall share with you. Wherever I sleep, you are welcome to a share of my blanket. And you will have a corner of my room and rest upon a velvet cushion."

That is why, in certain parts of Ashantiland to this day, cats are pampered and petted while dogs receive the remnants of affection and the left-overs of food.

D4